Beneath a Star-Blue Sky

Seven Tales of Love and Grace

Beneath a Star-Blue Sky

Seven Tales of Love and Grace

by

William Woodall

Jeremiah Press · *Antoine, Arkansas*

Jeremiah Press
PO Box 121
Antoine, AR 71922
www.jeremiahpress.org

First published by Jeremiah Press on 02/11/2009.

Printed in the United States of America.

This book is printed on acid-free paper.

ISBN 978-0-9819641-3-3

Library of Congress Control Number: 2009920153

For Nathan, Elisabeth, Mathew,
Cody, Zach, and Brandon,

For listening to these tales,
And thinking they were good ones.

Other Books by William Woodall:

The Prophet of Rain

Cry for the Moon

Contents

The Keeper of Songs

A Tale of Love

Heard melodies are sweet,
But those unheard are sweeter.

-John Keats

The Keeper of Songs

Once there was a King who betrayed all his people for love, and once there was a boy who never forgot. The King was Ulysses; the boy had no name, for he was not meant to ever need one.

It was whispered that the King wept bitterly for twelve days and twelve nights when his first child was born, for even the servants could see what a strong and laughing youth he would be, the fairest there ever had been in all the land of Colmar.

The Queen his mother had begged not to see or touch him, and the King took pity on his wife, and took the child away the moment he was born. They had spent many sad months preparing for this day, and the King fed and cared for the baby with his own hands. He dared not allow anyone else.

When the first fair day arrived (for it was in the rainy autumn-time when the child was born), the King mounted a donkey with his baby son held in a sling across his heart, and bid his Queen and his palace farewell. The Queen would rule Colmar until his return, and that would be many years away. In the meantime the babe was his only concern.

The King rode away to the cottage prepared for him, deep in the Wilds where none other dared go, on pain of death. And there they remained always. The young King turned his strength to growing food and he put away thoughts of sorrow, for they were forbidden here.

The child grew, and was as fair and merry as his midwives had thought, and in him the King found much joy. And each day the King took the boy by the hand, and led him through fields where the red clover grew, by a silvery stream that played over rocks, and under the leaves of the old oak trees that danced in the wind and the sun. And the little one smiled at these things that he saw, and hid them away in his heart.

Then at last, every day, they came to a hill, where the sweet grass flowed in a cool green wave whenever the breeze came along. There at the top stood a cabin of wood, and inside it the Stone of Possibilities. So said the King, and the little one believed him, though never, not *once,* did they open the door.

"Someday you will enter that door, little child, and that day will break my heart," the King said to him once, one fine summer's day. (for the days were all fine, in that time.)

"Oh, no, Papa, never!" the little boy cried, for he couldn't have borne to cause such a sorrow, and he loved his Papa most dearly. He promised with childish conviction, but after a moment the King looked down, fingering the necklace of silver he wore.

"No, child, that is a promise you mustn't ever make, for this is the thing you were born for. Promise me only this much; remember!"

And the little boy never forgot.

Each day the King would tell stories, there on the hill in the woods, of wisdom and truth and love long ago, and he filled his child's head with dreams. And all of these were sweet as mint, for all of them were true. And each day also the man would sing (and no two Songs were ever alike), while the little one listened in wonder. When twilight came, just one word was spoken, and that was the word "Remember."

And the little boy never forgot.

Then at last a day came, after many golden years, when all the world changed. It was a crisp and whispering day in the fall when the boy was twelve years old, and the brown oak leaves fluttered and danced on the path in the sun as they walked. The boy smiled at these things, as he always did, and remembered, and squeezed his Papa's hand.

They came to the hill where the sweet grass flowed in a soft green wave in the breeze, and here the King stopped, and turned to the boy, and took both his hands in his own.

"Today I must leave you," the King said softly.

"But Papa, where are you going?" the little one asked. He couldn't imagine such a thing, for his Papa had *never* been away.

"In there," his father told him, and nodded his head at the cabin. The cabin with only the Stone inside. The boy thought about this and finally smiled, for that was his way in those days.

"Then I will wait for you here, even if it takes all day," he said. But his father looked sad, which astonished the boy. . . he had seldom known sorrow, either.

"You misunderstand, child. I can never come back to you, ever again. Listen closely to every word I say," the King said urgently, gripping the boy's hands tight enough to hurt. He dropped to his knees and looked not only sad but fearful, and the boy began to be uneasy. But he listened all the same, and never forgot.

"Child, you must run from this place as fast as you can. Don't dare to slow down or look back. Never tell anyone where you came from, or how you were raised, or mention my name. If they knew who you were, they would kill you at once. We were forbidden to give you a name, but you will need one now. So, I name you Nathan, for you have been a gift to me, and I pray you will be so to many others." At this point he reached in his pocket and took out a rough black stone, which he pressed into Nathan's palm.

"This is a piece of the Stone of Possibilities. Keep it safe, and never tell anyone you have it. It will give you great power, for I have sung to you the dreams of everyone in Colmar. Remember them all, and be wise, child. You were born to be a gift for the people; be a greater one now than they ever expected. Save them from Jòkai, and the Curse of Blood."

Now Nathan was frightened and clung to his father, and there on the hill he whispered "Don't go."

"Child, I must," his father said.

"But *why?*" Nathan cried.

"If I stayed, the cost would be too much to bear. I cannot tell you more than that. Now let me go, my Nathan. You are all I ever loved or wanted. . . Run now, and God keep you safe!" the

King said. He brushed away the hair from the boy's brow and kissed him just once, very tenderly, then without another word he turned and walked away. Nathan stood frozen to the spot as the King approached the cabin and opened the door. Then he was gone.

"I promise, Papa. . . I'll try," Nathan whispered.

A minute later the piece of rock in his hand grew hot as blood, and a hard gust of wind almost sent him sprawling. He scrambled to his feet and caught sight of black clouds rushing down from the north beyond the mountains, and with no more hesitation he ran off the hill and away. He passed the forest of oaks where the branches groaned and snapped in the rising wind, and the silvery stream that played over rocks, and the meadow that once had been full of red clover. Then the rain came, heavy and blinding, and Nathan could see no more. He was soaked through in an instant. He dared not stop at the little cottage where he had spent his whole life, for just then the lightning began. He heard thunder and knew the bolt had struck somewhere behind him in the forest. Then the crash came again, and again, till the sound overlapped in a long rolling roar so loud it seemed his very ears would bleed. He covered them with his hands while he ran.

He ran for what felt like hours, not knowing where he was going or why; just running because he must. At last the storm grew less, and the lightning and wind died away. The rain became a drizzle, then even that stopped. The woods were quiet except for the crunch of his footsteps on wet leaves and bracken, and the drip of soaked bark. Nathan shivered, for it had turned cold in the wake of the storm, and he was not dry yet. He trudged on in silence, lonely and afraid and beginning to feel hungry. Already he missed his Papa.

All day long he walked without seeing any hint of people. He drank water from clear pools where it had collected after the rain, but there was nothing to eat except a few stray nuts the squirrels had missed. Near dusk he came upon a fallen log, and used his bare hands to tear away fistfuls of rotten wood till he reached the dry interior. He snuggled into the depression he had made and buried himself in the torn up pieces. They picked up a little of the heat from his body and kept him warm. It was still early, but Nathan closed his eyes and slept, too tired to think.

When he opened them he was cold as the kiss of the frost, but early morning sunlight streamed down through the branches to wash him with pale warmth. He rose from his bed and drank more water, then set off at once, ignoring his hunger. At midmorning he came to a road.

It was nothing but a muddy country lane, but to Nathan it seemed salvation. He fell to his knees and let out a cry of joy, the red clay sticking to the cloth of his breeches.

With fresh hope he followed the little road east; not because it would take him to any real end, but just that it allowed him to face the warm sun. Beyond that his thoughts were still vague.

By and by the trees thinned, and he began to pass fields golden yellow and ripe with the harvest, and pretty old farm houses scattered about. And these things were marvelous, amazing to behold.

"Ho, boy," a voice called, and Nathan was startled. It was the first voice he'd ever heard except his Papa's and his own. He looked all around.

There on the ground by a moss-covered apple tree sat a girl. She was older than he was, maybe sixteen or so. Nathan stared at her, lost in curiosity. He was conscious of rudeness, but couldn't seem to help it. He didn't know quite what to say.

"What's your name?" the girl asked, when the silence had grown too long.

"I'm . . . Nathan," he told her, the name sounding strange on his lips. It was the first time he had ever yet uttered it.

"Just Nathan, that's all?" she smiled. He couldn't reply; only yesterday he'd lacked even that much. He shrugged.

"Well, Nathan, I'm Cynthia, and if you're not in a hurry I hope you'll sit down and have lunch with me. You're the first one I've seen on this road all day long," she said. Nathan was happy to take up her offer. She reached in her pack and brought out bread and cheese, which she cut into slices for both of them. At first they said little. "Where are you from?" she'd ask. (That way.) "Then where are you headed?" (Don't know.) Cynthia finally became exasperated.

"Did you just fall out of the sky then, boy?" she asked. He could tell she expected no answer to that, and he wisely didn't offer her one. They sat there in the quiet for a while, and the girl absentmindedly began to hum a little tune. Something clicked in Nathan's mind, and he knew this girl instantly for who she was. The sudden knowledge made him gasp.

"What is it, Nathan?" she asked, concerned. She half rose, to put out a hand to his cheek.

"You're the great singer!" he exclaimed with delight, for he remembered his Papa telling him about her, long ago. He almost went on to say something more, but he noticed the way she was staring.

"I'm headed for the City to study my music," she said to him slowly, "All of my life I've dreamed of the day when I'd sing at the court of the Queen, but how did *you* know that?"

Nathan was speechless again, but knew she wouldn't simply let it drop. She was much too determined for that. He knew more about her than she knew about herself, and realized he would have to say *something*. He muttered a word or two under his breath.

"What's that?" she prodded, leaning toward him expectantly. He held back another minute, then told her a bit of the truth.

"I know a Song about you," he confessed.

"A song about *me?*" she asked, amused.

"Yes. It's a very beautiful Song," Nathan told her. And this was certainly true, for all the Songs were beautiful.

The girl smiled prettily, and because he wished to please her he opened his mouth to sing. He sang her own Song, which his Papa had taught him on the hill in the woods where the sweet grass flowed in a soft green wave in the breeze. He sang of all that was true and good inside her, of her deepest hopes and dreams, and everything she had ever loved. He captured her soul in his Song, and never saw her tears till the music was done. Then he noticed.

"What-" he began, but she cut him off sharply.

"Why did you tell me!" she screamed in rage and grief, and he pulled back from her hastily, scared. What had he done to her? She tore at her hair and her clothes, and her body shrank as he watched until nothing was left but a bright blue pebble that sat upon the ground by the tree.

A pale sparrow alighted nearby and looked up at Nathan with steady black eyes, full of death and unspeakable cold. With a dart of its head it swallowed the stone, then departed as quickly as it came.

Here was Nathan's first sorrow, and the beginning of wisdom. No one could bear to know his own soul too well.

And Nathan never forgot.

For days he wandered the old country roads. He took Cynthia's pack rather than leave it by the road, but the food was soon gone. Then he starved. Sometimes he passed people who would give him a crust or even a meal, but more often not. It was lonely country, so near to the Wilds. He became very weak, as time went on. At first he didn't know what was wrong when the coughing and fever came over him. He'd never been sick before. He was frightened again and searched through his memories till he found one of a man who might help.

He came to a place where the land fell away in high cliffs to the sea, and many bright birds called and soared in the sere blue sky. And here on the close cropped grass stood an ancient old man, weathered and cracked as the stones down below. His name was Timias, and he was a hermit, a seeker after wisdom and knowledge. He was a kindly soul, and would understand what to do. All this Nathan knew, and he knew also that no other healer lived in this desolate region. The hermit was his only chance. He stumbled out of the forest and fell at the side of the path, and for many days he knew no more.

When he woke he was lying in a bed, and the old man Timias stood close beside him, with something that steamed in a bowl.

"I thought you would wake soon," the man whispered in a papery voice, "You've been very ill, child. . . you must eat something now."

Nathan had no strength to reply, but he opened his mouth just a little. The old man fed him with a carved wooden spoon, as if he were a baby, till all the broth was gone. Then he slept again. Many more days passed in this way.

At last a morning came when the chill winds of November rattled like ghosts around the eaves of the house, and Nathan sat up in bed and knew he was well. Timias' care had saved him. He was still not too strong, but he knew that would pass in time.

The year was growing late, and winter could be cruel to those unprepared. When Timias heard that Nathan was alone, he refused to let him leave until spring. Nathan was grateful, and spent the long winter in the old hermit's house. It became a pleasant habit to sit before the fire in the long nights together, for Timias was wise and had many tales to tell which Nathan had never heard. He spoke of wytches and ghosts, and evil things that walked the moors by night and drank the blood of babes asleep; such things as terrified a boy who had never heard a falsehood in his life. But he kept his fear inside, for he noticed that in all the stories Timias told, the good and the right overcame the dark and the evil in the end, terrible as the monsters might be. That gave him courage.

The most terrible stories were of Jòkai the Dark One, who dwelt in the cold north beyond the mountains. Even Timias' voice betrayed a tremble when he spoke of the Dark One, for this story was real.

"He is the spiritual vampire, child. He feeds upon pain and terror, and especially does he love to drink the blood of the innocent. Once he came often into Colmar by night and filled all our land with horror and death. But we made a pact with him long ago, little Nathan. He cannot hurt us now," Timias promised. Nathan's curiosity was aroused, but Timias would say no more about the Dark One then.

Sometimes Timias did speak of nobler things, or read from his books, and there were memories, memories, always memories. In this way Timias reminded Nathan of his Papa, and he grew to love the old man. So it was that just before the first pale buds of spring appeared on the trees by the path, Nathan confessed to him all that had happened and all that he knew, in spite of his father's warning. Timias was silent for a long while. When he spoke again his voice was cold.

"If I had known, I would have taken your Stone and cut your throat where you fell upon the path," Timias said, staring into the depths of the fire. At Nathan's sudden look of horror the old man waved a weary hand.

"No, sit down, boy; I won't harm you. It wouldn't do any good *now*. The time is past, and you have learned too much. Your father has destroyed the world, and nothing can undo it. You might as well live. Much good may it do you," Timias said bitterly, and then cursed King Ulysses in the foulest terms possible. Nathan trembled on the verge of tears.

"But Timias, *why?* Papa wouldn't tell me; I don't understand!" he begged. Timias sighed.

"Your father had a silver necklace he always wore, did he not?"

Nathan agreed that he had.

"That was his Scepter; a gift of Jòkai to the kings of our land. With it, your father looked deep into the hearts of all his subjects, and then taught you all the good things he found there. And this he did, so that when the autumn of your twelfth year came, he might spill your blood upon the Stone of Possibilities and cause all that you remembered to come true. There is great power in the blood, boy. That was our pact with the Dark One. One pure and innocent life as a sacrifice for him to devour; in return he would grant the heart's desire of all others in Colmar. Just one sacrifice in each generation, but if ever we fail to give it then Jòkai will come ravening as a wolf from the north to devour us all and utterly destroy our land forever. Why do you think Ulysses taught you so many joyful things, and showed you only goodness? And now he has let you go, and turned all our hopes into ashes." The vicious hatred in the old man's voice was unmistakable.

"Get out!" Timias screamed harshly, raising a clenched fist as he jumped to his feet. Nathan leaped from his chair and fled the house in tears, for even by that time he had never dreamed that such hatred could exist.

But all this too, Nathan never forgot.

He walked alone and shivering in the cold light of late winter, and the wind cut cruelly through his thin indoor clothing. He wept for a time at the evil of the world, but soon gave that up. It did him no good. And as he walked he pondered. At first he refused to believe his Papa had ever meant to kill him, but he couldn't deceive himself for long. Self deception was not easy, for one who remembered every word his father had ever spoken. He recalled his Papa talking of the day when Nathan would enter the cabin, and how it would break the King's heart when it happened. Now Nathan knew why. He wept afresh at that, to think his Papa had so coldly planned his death on the Stone. . . but he also knew that in the end his Papa hadn't done it. What did that mean? And why, without a sacrifice, had not Jòkai already destroyed all Colmar?

Nathan froze in place, for he suddenly had a terrible suspicion. Only one other person besides Nathan could be the sacrifice, for only one other person knew the Songs. And *someone* must have died, or Jòkai would have long since put an end to all stories.

"Oh, Papa. . . no," Nathan whispered. But even as he denied it, he knew it must be so. That was a grief he couldn't yet face. Then a new thought crossed his mind. His Papa had known not only the good things in his people (which was all he had ever taught Nathan), but also the horrible and selfish and evil things. Not only what they hoped for, but also what they feared. And if that were true, then Timias' frightening stories might now be something more than just stories. Nathan shivered again, not entirely from the cold.

He came to a farmstead, lips blue and toes numb, and was given his supper and a place by the stove to sleep. It was the home of a yeoman and his wife, who lived all alone and had enough to spare. He would not be a hardship on anyone. In the morning they fed him again and gave him a cloak, then sent him gently on his way. But before he had gone too far, he stopped for a moment to think. He knew their Songs, and and knew that what they both wanted most was a baby. They had been married for years, and almost given up hope. Nathan fingered the piece of Stone in his pocket and wondered if Timias had told him the truth. Power in the blood, but only his, since no other knew the Songs. He took out the Stone and speculatively removed the pin of his cloak. If it took *all* his blood to satisfy everyone's wishes, might just a drop of it suffice for one couple? Let Jòkai have a taste of what he thirsted for; perhaps it would make the Dark One greedy for more, and thus easier to destroy when the time came. Nathan wasn't sure where that coldly logical thought had come from, or even when he had firmly decided he must destroy Jòkai, but he had not forgotten his promise.

With the pin from his cloak he pricked his left thumb, and bled two drops of blood upon the stone. They vanished at once and the Stone grew warm in his hand. Then, quietly lest someone hear, he sang the two Songs of the farmer and his wife. When he finished the Stone was cold. Had it worked? He might never know.

Thoughtfully he replaced the Stone in his pocket, and refastened the cloak about his throat. His left thumb hurt and he put it in his mouth till the wind slicing in through the slit in his cloak grew too cold to endure, then he pulled his hand inside and clasped it fully shut. With a smile that was almost sad, he set off again through the snowy woods.

For months Nathan wandered alone, and he saw many things that grieved him, and much that was hateful and cruel. Things that contradicted the Songs in his memory, and so he knew they would never have come to be if he had been the one to die on the Stone. He didn't need to know the dark side of his people anymore; he was seeing it in real life. And if ever he dared to utter his Papa's name he was invariably met with a curse or a blow. He learned quickly to keep what he knew to himself. Sometimes as he travelled he took out the Stone, and spilled a few drops of his blood upon it to make someone's dreams come true, or at least to wash away some terrible hurt. He kept this most stringently secret, never saying a word to the ones he helped, and quickly moving on before anyone could notice him.

But among those he touched, some did see, and remembered. Not many, or often, but these spread the tale. A story grew up wherever he went. People murmured that it was luck to catch sight of him, a blessing to touch his cloak. Those who had given up hope when they heard what Ulysses had done now dared to imagine that Nathan might find them. How they came to know his name Nathan never could guess, but he smiled to himself all the same.

And the Queen in her citadel heard all these tales, and wondered how much was true. She thought of the husband she had not seen for twelve years, and knew who the boy must be. Her son. She quietly ordered her folk not to harm him, with a bittersweet taste in her mouth, though fear was wrapped close around her heart. The Dark One was not to be cheated so lightly.

And deep in the Wilds, on a day in late summer when the cold and the dark seemed farthest away, Nathan decided that the time had come when Jòkai must be destroyed. He knew only that the Dark One dwelt far in the north, in the ice and the stone where nothing could live. How to seek out and conquer him, the boy did not know, but neither did any other in Colmar. He would learn nothing by waiting any longer. Though far from unafraid, Nathan gathered his courage and took the northern road.

For days he walked and saw no one. Few people cared to live in the shadow of the northern mountains. But the road went on, climbing steeply upward, and then passed into a narrow gorge between two high cliffs. A chill breeze blew out and wafted the fringe of Nathan's hair. Inside was dusky twilight, never touched by the sun. Nathan stopped to pull his cloak around his shoulders, and prayed for the strength to do whatever he must. Then, his courage renewed, he plunged into the dark. It closed about him eagerly, and when he turned the first corner the bright summer world was lost.

The crack twisted and turned unpredictably with no rhyme or reason, but it was much shorter than Nathan had expected. Abruptly the walls fell away on both sides, and he stood at the top of a slope strewn with ice. It glittered pale blue in the weak sun that filtered from the heavy gray clouds above. There was no wind, no blade of grass, not a single living thing that Nathan could see. Just the empty, cold landscape that stretched on forever, and the dreary mountains at his back. He was come into the place of the Dark One.

The road faded out on the rock-littered plain, not far from the foot of the hill. Nathan hesitated briefly, then followed it down. He crept on past where the road left off, picking his way among the fragments of stone. The sound of his breathing seemed loud in the silence.

The boulders blocked his sight, and he stopped to climb up and look around from the top of one. It was cold enough to freeze the light moisture on his fingertips, causing them to stick to the surface. He reached the flat top and saw that the road had nearly vanished behind him. If he ever once lost it, he was not at all sure he could find it again. He dared not go farther.

"Jòkai, I am here!" he cried at the top of his voice. Weird echoes rebounded from the mountains behind before dying very slowly away, and Nathan sat down on the rock to wait for the Dark One to find him.

And the Dark One came.

A glimmer of motion at the northern horizon soon caught Nathan's eye and swiftly drew closer. In the blink of an eye an old man stood before him. His garb was of purest white, with long hair and beard the color of mist, and eyes as black as night. In his right hand he held a small pebble of blue.

"You have sent me a soul out of turn, King of Colmar," the white figure said, in a voice as quiet and cold as the snow. He held up the pebble and dropped it into Nathan's palm.

"She cannot live in My realm. Take her to the mouth of the cleft and she will then be restored," Jòkai told him. He did not seem to care at all that Nathan had once been his chosen prey not very long before. He reached into a fold of his robe and withdrew a silver necklace. Nathan recognized it at once, for it was the one his Papa had worn.

"Your Scepter, King," the Dark One murmured, and made as if to place the chain around Nathan's neck.

"I do not accept it; I reject the treaty of my ancestors," Nathan said, hoping that his voice sounded firm. Jòkai was silent for a very long while, and never blinked.

"You have not the authority to do this. Our pact is signed in blood, eternal. You may refuse the Scepter if you choose, but without it you cannot prepare My sacrifice. And if you do not, then when the time comes I will drink the blood of all Colmar. Many great kings have thought to refuse our treaty, in the unthinking days of youth. All of them accepted in the end. For the sake of the people they took up the burden of the King, to provide My sacrifice. Do you likewise."

"You lie," said Nathan coldly, "My father hated the Curse every day of his life, and in the end he turned his back on you."

"Nay... he merely substituted one sacrifice for another. That is all one to Me, little King. If it pleases you, do the same when your own time comes. You dare not refuse Me." With that, Jòkai slipped the Scepter over Nathan's head before the boy could prevent it. The touch of his fingers as they brushed Nathan's cheek was cold enough to burn.

Nathan gasped, for it seemed that now he saw deep into the soul of every man and woman in Colmar, all at once. It was like ten thousand Songs pouring into his mind; a waterfall, an avalanche of music. But these were not all like the beautiful ones his Papa had sung to him. There were some of those, but there were evil strains in these Songs as well. Unworthy desires, cold cruelties, terrible fears and hatreds. Nathan clutched his head in pain, and tears slipped down his cheeks to freeze on the black rock. Through it all came the cold voice of the Dark One, sharp as a stiletto, piercing the confusion.

"You see, Boy? See them for what they really are. You grieved for the pain and hurt you saw in the land. Know then, foolish one, every bit of it they inflicted upon each other, because of the evil desires of their hearts. Your father set that evil free when he took your place, and nothing will change it until the next sacrifice is made. Go

back to Colmar, King. Give your firstborn to Me
as all your forefathers did, and bring happiness
back to your people. It is not such a great price to
pay, unless your heart is too weak to bear it. Great
Kings are not broken by sentiment when the fate
of their country is at stake, and this you well
know. In times past, Colmar has been the fairest
and most joyful land in all the world. It can be so
again," Jòkai urged.

For a moment Nathan was almost swayed
by the Dark One's logic and the power of his
voice. Was one life worth more than ten
thousand? Was it right to condemn a whole
nation for the sake of one person, who would then
die anyway when Jòkai destroyed them all?
Nathan could hardly think for the haze of pain in
his head. Yet he knew that he held the future of
his people in his hands. He must act with all
Colmar in mind, not simply himself, nor even his
possible firstborn child. Only the kingdom, and
its flawed and unhappy people. Nathan felt for
the first time the loneliness of power.

With an effort he shut out the wailing of the
Songs and composed himself. Without the music

pouring in, his mind cleared. He took a deep breath of the cold air and looked Jòkai in the eye.

"You are right, Dark One. My people are weak and evil, and cause themselves much sorrow by it. I could indeed go back to rule them wisely, and make your sacrifice upon the Stone of Possibilities. Perhaps it would be worth it. I could make them happy, and save them from death. Many have made that choice before me... but still I will not do it," Nathan said. A smile had begun to creep across the Dark One's thin lips, but at Nathan's final word it vanished at once.

"Why not, then?" he asked.

"Because you lie!" Nathan cried, "Indeed, your gifts are more bitter than dying. By your curse every good and noble dream my people imagine is twisted into a bitter and empty husk, tainted with blood-guilt. You offer happiness, but in fact you rob them of all pure joy. Perhaps they had very little of that before, but now they have none at all. That has ended today, Dark One. You may come and destroy us, but you will never corrupt us again."

And Jòkai was filled with anger and hate for the boy-King of Colmar who dared to defy him.

"You will not break our treaty if you are not there to lead, Boy. Another may wear the Scepter as easily as you." And Jòkai curled his fingers into claws as sharp as serpents' teeth, and reached out his long arm for Nathan's throat. He would have his blood after all.

Nathan felt a sharp bolt of terror, but then did the only thing he could think of. He snatched the Stone of Possibilities from his pocket and swiftly raked it across his palm. A thin line of bright red welled up. Nathan gripped the Stone with that hand, ignoring the stinging pain from the cut. Then, for the last time in his life, he used the power of the Scepter.

He looked straight into the heart of the Thing standing before him. He saw only a black emptiness, a pit that could never be filled, a hunger that nothing exist at all. Nathan gagged as if he'd tasted something vile, but he opened his mouth and forced his lips to sing the terrible Song of Jòkai. The stone grew blood-warm in his hand, and a coldness began to creep up his arm. The

Stone was still drinking from him; even now, the Dark One thirsted. The flesh of the boy's forearm became the color of bleached bone, and his head grew light and fuzzy, but somehow he kept up the Song. He must not fail, even if it killed him.

When the last note was finished, Jòkai's shrieks cut off sharply, and there on the dirt lay a bright black pebble. The Stone of Possibilities slipped from Nathan's hand and fell to the ground with a soft thud, where it crumbled into dust. Nathan smiled faintly and whispered, "It is done, Papa." Then he slumped forward.

When he woke, many hours later, he could barely move and felt only half alive. His skin was cool and pale as milk, and he hurt all over. He reached down to pick up the black pebble that was the soul of Jòkai the Dark One, and began to make his slow and painful way back toward the cleft in the mountains.

A thin ray of light broke through the clouds to splash the cold ground, startling him. He looked up, and saw patches of summer blue through the dull grayness. He wondered at this, and then noticed the light breeze tickling his ears. A warm breeze. Jòkai's power was broken.

Slowly, the ghost of his old warm smile began to spread over Nathan's face, and his step was lighter for the rest of the way. As light as it had ever been on the path in the oak woods long ago, where the green leaves danced in the wind and the sun, and he held the hand of one who loved him more than life.

When he emerged from the mountain gorge and looked down into Colmar it seemed as if a great shadow had fallen away from the land, a shadow he had never known was there until it lifted. Every rock and tree looked bright and new; looked *free*.

Nathan laughed aloud and clapped his hands for joy. There would be much work to do; many, many years before the people could cast off completely the sickness Jòkai had woven about them. But in time, Colmar would be a richer and kinder land than it had ever been in the days of the Curse, if only the people would choose it. Nathan lifted his eyes to Heaven and thanked God for leading them aright, for he had faith that it would be so.

Then, smiling, he went down to join his people.

Singing Wind

A Tale of Courage

In beauty be it finished.

-Navajo proverb

Singing Wind

Long ago, there was a girl named Singing Wind, whose hair was the longest and blackest of all the girls in the village, and whose face was more beautiful than any of the others as well. Her people lived in a village on the Ikahiri Plain, and moved about from year to year to plant their crops in fresh soil. It was a good life, and Singing Wind was the happiest of them all.

But it happens at times that too much fame and beauty can lead to difficulties, and so it was with Singing Wind.

There was in those days a certain Witch named Alitha who lived alone in a hut in the woods, and in time the tale of the beauty of Singing Wind came to her ears. She was at once filled with a jealous rage, for although she was very ugly, she fancied herself the most beautiful lady in all the Plain. No one had ever dared to tell her otherwise, for she was much too powerful and dangerous for that.

She was able, when she chose, to transform herself into a hideous monster that no one dared to fight. Alitha could become a dead skull with glowing eyes that rolled about and spewed forth coals and flame to burn anything that came near her to ashes.

And so it was that Alitha walked into the village one day, and demanded to be taken to the headman's house. The people dared not refuse, for they knew who she was. The Witch and the fear of her had gone wide throughout the lands.

When she came to the headman's house, Alitha got right to the point.

"Headman, I know you have a girl in your village by the name of Singing Wind, said by some to be beautiful. You will bring her here immediately, and she will come to live with me, and then you and your people must depart from this place immediately and go to live far away," the Witch commanded him. The headman was considered brave, and his warriors also, but none of them dared to say no to the Witch, for they knew she could lay waste to the entire village and reduce them all to ashes if she chose.

Therefore the headman sent for Singing Wind, and told her what must be, that she should go to live with the Witch. Singing Wind wept and tore her clothes, but there was no help, for she saw that the headman would not resist the evil one. Therefore she calmed herself, and arose from her seat, and spoke to the headman calmly.

"Sir, if I'm to go with the Witch, there are three things I'll have to take with me," she told him.

"You can't take any weapons, nor anything valuable," the headman warned her. Singing Wind agreed to this, and fetched a small bundle from a shelf in the house. Then she went with the headman to the front of his hut.

When the Witch saw the beauty of Singing Wind, she was amazed, but her heart was filled all the more with hatred and spite. She opened the bundle that Singing Wind had brought, but it contained only a plum twig, a small bottle of water, and a mussel shell. The Witch cared nothing for these things and allowed her to keep them. Then she took the girl to her own hut, after remaining long enough to make certain that the people of the village had fled far away.

And so Singing Wind was left alone with her tormentor. For the Witch was very hateful, and heaped all manner of cruelties upon Singing Wind whenever she could. She would frequently stab her with sharp thorns when she passed close by, or force her to rake up hot coals with her bare hands so that her skin was burned and blackened. She refused to allow her to ever wash her hair or to bathe in the stream close by, or to make new clothes for herself. In the fall when the hut was invaded by hideous black roaches, Alitha forced her to eat them. In this way the Witch hoped to destroy Singing Wind's beauty and turn her into a bitter and fearful slave. Alitha threatened her that if she ever tried to escape, that she would hunt her down and burn her to ashes, along with anyone who dared to help her.

Singing Wind pretended to be terrified of the Witch, and in truth she did fear her, but she had courage, and refused to give up the idea of escaping and returning to her people. And although she was forced to live in filth and cruelty, she was just as beautiful as she had always been, for true beauty shines from the heart, like a fire that can never be put out.

Now it happened by and by that the Witch had business of her own to attend to in other parts, and she wished to go off on her own for a time. However, she was gripped by the fear that Singing Wind might take this chance to try to escape her, and she was determined that this should not happen.

Therefore the Witch announced her intention to leave, and again threatened Singing Wind with horrible consequences if she dared set foot beyond the vicinity of the hut. Then the Witch pretended to depart, but in fact she went only a short distance from the hut and hid herself behind a tree to see what her prisoner would do.

Singing Wind was no fool, and she continued to do her work about the yard and the hut, without so much as a glance towards the deep woods where she might try to escape. After a time, the Witch was satisfied that Singing Wind would not dare to leave the hut, and she departed to take care of her other business.

Singing Wind waited for a time, until she was certain that the Witch was far away, and then she acted quickly. She gathered her bundle of possessions, and departed from the Witch's hut immediately.

She was not so foolish as to think she would be able to escape from the Witch without help, and so she headed at once for the den of a certain Bear who lived not far away and who might be able to protect her.

It was not long before Singing Wind approached the home of the Bear, and as she came to his den she called aloud to him.

"Oh, great Bear, I'm in terrible trouble, for a powerful monster is after me, and there's no one who can help me but you," she cried. And the

Bear heard her plea, and lumbered out slowly to meet her. He looked upon her beauty, and he was inclined in his heart to help her. Therefore he said,

"Tell me then, lass. . . what's this monster you fear? I'll crush it with one flick of my little claw," he boasted, and held up his paw. And Singing Wind was glad, for she thought the Bear would save her.

"Great Bear, I'm being chased by the evil Witch Alitha, and if you hadn't helped me then I would have been lost," she thanked him. But the Bear was startled when he heard that name, and a new attitude came over his face.

"Ah, no! Not the Witch! For she will set fire to my fur and burn me to ashes, and you along with me! Great though I am, I dare not fight against the Witch. But go to the Mountain Lion, and perhaps he may be able to help you. Now go!" the Bear ordered her, his eyes bulging in terror. And he turned tail and hid himself deep in his den.

Singing Wind hid her fear, and would not give up. She wasted no time on the Bear anymore, but set out at once for the cave of the Mountain Lion, in the hope that he might be more brave.

In the meantime the Witch had returned from her trip sooner than Singing Wind had thought, and she flew into a rage when she found the girl gone. She muttered her curses and took her skull shape, and her wicked red eyes glowed fiercely with hate. She suspected the Bear at once, and set off to see him, for she was determined that the girl should not escape.

She came to the den of the Bear before long, for she could roll very swiftly when she needed to.

"Have you seen a young girl pass this way, old Bear? Tell me at once, or I'll burn you to ashes, you filthy old flat-foot," she demanded. And the Bear stuck the tip of his nose from his cave, and in a voice that trembled he answered her back.

"Yes, I've seen her. She asked me for help, but I gave none. She headed that way, toward the cave of the Lion," he told her in fear, pointing his paw toward the west.

"Hah," the Witch grumbled, and paid no more mind, rolling off quickly.

So fast did she roll, it was not very long till she saw Singing Wind just ahead, and she laughed to herself, spewing coals all about.

Singing Wind heard the monster and said nothing else, but she reached into her bag and pulled out the plum twig. She broke it in half, and threw the pieces down behind her. At once there arose such a thick, tangled mass of thorny plum trees that she knew it would take the skull quite some time to burn its way through. And in the meantime she came to the cave of the Mountain Lion.

She stopped, out of breath, and called to him quickly.

"Great Lion, please help me! A terrible monster is hot on my heels, and no one can save me but you," she cried out. And the Mountain Lion blinked in the bright noonday sun, and Singing Wind's beauty was such that he decided to help her. Therefore he said,

"And what is this poor puny monster you fear? Why, I could crush it with one flick of my little claw," he told her, and held up his paw. But Singing Wind hesitated, for she remembered the Bear.

"Great Lion, the Witch named Alitha is coming, and- " she began, but the Cat cut her off. A look of bright terror came over his face.

"The Witch will burn both of us right down to ashes! There's nothing I can do against a monster like that! But go to the Snake, and perhaps he will help you. I dare not. Now go!" the Cat said, and fled into his cave.

Singing Wind was frightened, but she still kept on, for what else could she do except wait for the skull?

In the meantime the Witch had burned her way through the thicket, and came to the cave of the Mountain Lion.

"Milk licker! Where has that ugly girl gone, for I know she came here to see you!" the Witch demanded.

And the Lion poked only his nose from his cave, and with trembling and terror he answered the Witch.

"She went that way, oh great one, to see the old Snake. I gave her no help, I promise!" he cried. The Witch said no more to the Cat, and rolled off, and before long she had almost caught up with her prey.

"Now I've got you!" she cried, coming close indeed. But Singing Wind reached for her bundle, and pulled out the bottle of water inside. She poured it all out on the path right behind her, and at once there arose a wide lake between them. The lake was so wide, and so icy and deep, that she knew it would take quite some time to get around it. That gave her time to get to the Snake.

Before too much longer, the girl reached a place where a deep hole was dug, and that, she thought, must be where the Snake lived.

"Great Snake, there's no one to save me but you, for a monster is chasing me that no one can resist," she cried. And the Snake heard her cries, and slithered swiftly to meet her. He hissed when he saw her, her beauty was so great, and he thought he would help her, if only for that.

"So tell me, then. . . what is this poor little monster you fear? I will crush it with one flick of my tail," he boasted, and rattled his tine. And Singing Wind was happy, for the Snake seemed sure. But she thought of the Bear and the Cat, and she feared.

"Great Snake, the evil Witch Alitha has followed me here, and unless you destroy her I fear all is lost," she told him.

"Sss, no!" the Snake hissed, "Not the Witch! She will roast me for supper and burn you to ashes! You are lost!" the Snake told her, and dived underground.

Singing Wind was in terror now, for there was nowhere else to go, and before long the Witch would overtake her. But she still kept on, for what else could she do?

Indeed, before long the old Witch rolled up close, laughing and spewing her burning hot coals.

And Singing Wind reached in her bag one more time, to take out the very last thing that she had, and that was the mussel shell, shiny and white. She crushed the shell and threw it behind her, and at once the ground was covered with glittering diamonds, so many and so bright that the Witch could not count them.

She was sure of catching the girl at that point, so she stopped there awhile and took her own form. She picked up the diamonds as fast as she could, but there were so many it took quite some time. And then when she finally picked them all up, she found a little bag in the folds of her dress to put them inside, and the bag she hid in the hole of a tree, where it would be safe till she came back for it later. Then at last she took form as a skull once again, and rolled off after the girl she hated.

Singing Wind at last had come to a river, and it blocked her way forward completely. It was too wide to swim and too deep to wade, and at last she despaired of escaping.

But at the edge of the river she spied a tall boy, and not far down the bank was a solid wood hut. She had nothing to lose, and no time to think, so she went to the handsome young man.

"Boy, there's a monster that intends to destroy me, and none of the Beasts will help. Can you hide me awhile, till the monster is gone?" she pleaded.

And the boy saw her beauty, and he loved her at once, but he said nothing of that just yet.

"My name is Little Bear, and of course I will. Go inside the hut and hide under the bed, and if the monster does come then I'll kill it for you," he promised. Singing Wind didn't believe him, but took his advice, hoping to flee back the way she had come. The Witch might give up looking, sooner or later.

So she went in the hut and crawled under the bed, and there she waited for the skull to come. Little Bear stayed by the river outside, calm as can be, with a red wooden club in his hand.

In time the skull came, hateful and ugly, her eyes glowing red as hot coals. She saw the wide river and the tall young man, and Singing Wind nowhere in sight.

"Have you seen an ugly girl pass by, young man? If you have, tell me quickly which way did she go?" the Witch threatened, spitting out a few sparks.

Little Bear shrugged his strong shoulders a bit, either not scared at all or hiding it well.

"The girl is inside, and she is my guest. So turn tail and run, old Monster," he told her. The Witch was so shocked by this threat from the boy that at first she was speechless, but soon flew into a rage.

"Very well, then. I'll burn you both to ashes!" she screamed, and her eyes began to glow.

But before she could spew out her flaming hot coals, the boy raised the sacred red club high above her. And then, with one leap and a terrible cry, he smashed down the club between her eyes.

The skull cracked and shattered into a thousand small pieces, then Little Bear told his guest to come see.

Singing Wind stared at the broken up skull, all that was left of the terrible Witch, and then she looked back at the boy who had killed her.

"But how?" she asked wonderingly, touching a piece. She wondered, at first, if he was even truly human. For what normal man could have done such a thing?

"It was only a skull after all, you know. If you hit hard enough, it will break," he replied.

"But the Beasts were in terror, and my people as well," she insisted, still not quite believing it. Little Bear shrugged his shoulders.

"Ah, so was I, but I love you, you see, and how else was I ever to save you, if I lacked the courage to try?" he asked.

"You might have been killed, and us both burned to ashes," she said, but her heart was full.

"Maybe so, but we weren't, and I still love you dearly," he told her, with a practical smile. She laughed, for what else could she answer to that? So she took him with joy, and their love was deep.

Together they ground up the skull into powder, and burned it to ashes in a fire they built. In the spring they set out from that place by the river, and soon found her people not far across the Plain.

The people rejoiced at the story they told, and the death of the Witch filled them all with awe. The headman was shamed, for it was whispered among the huts that a boy and a girl had done what no leader ever dared.

In time all that people took Little Bear to lead them, and Singing Wind stood beside him in all that he did, and they lived many years in joy.

And in days long after, when they both slept with God, the people still remembered the tale of their deeds, till at last they are told here today.

Bran the Blessed

A Tale of Faith

May the sun shine warm upon your face,
the rain fall soft upon your fields,
and until we meet again,
may God hold you in the palm of His hand.

- Irish blessing

Bran the Blessed

Long ago, in a land by the sea, there came into the world a boy named Brandon. He was not so unusual to look at, and for a long time no one thought much about him one way or the other, except sometimes to remark how wonderfully well he got along with his sister.

The sister's name was Branwen, and these two loved each other very much, and they were never apart unless they had to be.

Their father herded sheep on the green grassy hills, and Brandon and Branwen did likewise as soon as they were old enough.

In those days the land had been at war for many years, till the people had almost forgotten what peace was like, and their hearts were heavy and sorrowful.

Now Branwen grew in time to be the most beautiful girl in all the land, and the kindest and gentlest of heart. And Brandon was beyond compare the bravest and strongest of all the young men.

So beautiful was Branwen, and so noble was Brandon, that even the King of Eyre heard tell of them in his castle across the sea, and he decided to set aside the war between their two lands, to come and see them both for himself.

So it was that on a day in the bright spring, King Lucas of Eyre came sailing across the sparkling sea with the wind at his back, and he first set foot on the beaches of Cambria in the early morning, with ten thousand nobles and soldiers beside him.

The people were terrified when they saw such an army encamped on the shore, and they hid themselves among the rocks of the mountains and dared not come out.

Of all the young men of Cambria that day, Brandon alone was not afraid, and he offered himself to walk down to the enemy's camp and talk to them. The others took courage when he said this, and so it was that three of them went with him to speak to King Lucas before noon.

But when they came within sight of the camp, the others lost heart and turned back, leaving Brandon to go on alone. He did so, and soon he came to the edge of the camp, where a soldier on guard called out to him.

"Who goes there?" he called, for he'd seen no one all day.

"My name is Brandon, and I've come to ask the King of Eyre the reason for his visit today," Brandon said to the man. Then the soldier smiled.

"That I can tell you already, young man. The King wished for only two things today, to speak to brave Brandon, and to see the sweet face of Branwen the Fair, for King Lucas has heard of them even in Eyre. Come in, and be welcome!" the soldier exclaimed. He sheathed his long sword and offered his hand, and Brandon allowed him to lead.

The camp was vast, a city of tents, and each one of them was full of the soldiers of Eyre. But Brandon stood tall in the camp that day, and the men of Eyre loved him for his courage, and gave him great honor. Before long he reached a tent of green and white silk where King Lucas sat on his great golden throne. The King stood to meet him, and Brandon knelt at his feet.

Lucas looked in his eyes long and hard, and whatever he saw there must have given him much to think about, for he didn't say a word to Brandon at all, and the silence was filled only with the sound of waves on the shore. At long last the King smiled, and asked Brandon to stand.

"I've seen the noble Brandon, and that was well worthy of coming. But now where is your sister, the beautiful Branwen? For I wish to see her before I leave, as well," he said.

"My sister has gone to the mountains to pray, and be safe from the battle we feared, Great King. But I can fetch her very quickly, if it pleases you to wait," Brandon offered, and the King smiled and nodded.

So Brandon departed from the camp for a while, to look for his sister in the mountains. He found her at last by the shores of Lake Miruvel, and their meeting was glad in the white morning mist.

"Where have you been, dear brother?" she cried, throwing her arms round his shoulders. He was happy as well, but no smile touched his face, for he knew there were serious things to discuss.

"I've spoken with King Lucas of Eyre. He tells me he wishes to see you, and for that reason he has crossed the sea with his men. He says he'll gladly return to his land, if only he can look on your beauty just once. It might be so, dear sister. But I fear he could change his mind when he sees you," he told her, and held her small hand.

Branwen considered these things, and finally she smiled to comfort his fear.

"That may be, dear brother. But in the meantime our land is in danger, and it might also be that this King is sincere. I'll go down and sing to him, and lull his heart, then maybe he'll leave us in peace," she said.

Then the two of them returned to the camp of King Lucas by the shore. The men were struck speechless by the beauty of Branwen, for it was greater by far than they had ever imagined. King Lucas too was amazed by the sight, and his tongue felt dry in his mouth when he spoke.

"I will never call anything lovely, nor ever see beauty on earth again, except in the face of Branwen," he declared when he finally spoke. She smiled at his words, and King Lucas loved her, forgetting everything else in the fire of his heart.

"Come with me, young maiden, and I'll make you a queen over all the land of Eyre beyond the whispering sea. And I'll never again make war on this land, the home of Branwen the beloved," he cried.

Then Branwen accepted, and the camp rejoiced, that peace should have come out of unexpected love.

The people feasted for weeks till the wedding was done. Then Branwen the Fair and Lucas the King embarked on his ship and departed for Eyre. And Brandon was happy, but sad as well, for he loved his sister very dearly.

For almost a year the news was good, and Branwen could only speak well of King Lucas. But then in the fall of the following year, no more letters came again across the bright wide sea. And Brandon feared only the worst.

Branwen was happy in Eyre at first, but in time her joy faded, for the women in the castle were jealous. None of them loved their new queen, not at all, and Lucas in time came to believe all their whispers. He began to find fault with his queen in small things, and then before long in larger ones too. At last all love had died in his heart, and he cast his wife into prison.

She found herself locked in a pig stye in rags, in the middle of winter forsaken and friendless. The women came to laugh and spit on her face, and only the pigs in the stye kept her warm. Her beauty was such that the King wouldn't kill her, but he kept her in prison while months rolled by.

But Branwen was faithful, and never lost heart, and she prayed to God every night in the snow, that somehow her brother might hear of her pain.

Then one evening as Branwen prayed, God sent a dream to Brandon while he slept. He saw his dear sister in rags in the mud, and then he heard her call out his name. He woke up in fear and put on his sword and his traveling clothes, for the dream was so strong that it couldn't be doubted. He set out for the shore by the light of the moon, for he could never rest a minute till he knew his sister was safe.

But no one would listen to Brandon's wild tale, and they told him to hush before his words caused a war. Not a single ship could he find that would carry him to Eyre, not for love nor money nor anything else. Brandon could plead for as long as he wished, but the hearts of the sailors were harder than stone.

Therefore Brandon fell down on his knees in the sand, and he begged the dear Lord for help, and he cared not at all who might see him.

Then God answered swiftly, and Brandon grew large. He grew till his head touched the clouds in the sky, and his feet shook the earth when he walked.

Then he went down and waded the cold gray sea, and God laid a calm on the wind and the waves till at last he set foot on the beaches of Eyre, and shrunk down again to his own normal size.

But the land was deserted when he reached the far shore, and he saw not a soul to help him.

For the people on the coast had seen him approaching, and in terror they hid from his sight. Word spread like wildfire that a giant was coming, who would crush every man in his path. So no one was left to see Brandon shrink down, or to know that the giant and he were the same.

He wandered alone for a very long time, for the land was wild and the people unfriendly, and no one would tell him the way he should go. But he never gave up, and his love never dimmed.

Finally then on a day in late spring, when the west winds blew and the bright sun shone, Brandon found his way at last to the castle of Lucas, and there he demanded to see the King.

The King was not pleased that Brandon had come, and pretended he was much too busy to talk. But Brandon was patient, and wouldn't go away, and he stood there for weeks by the gate. The whole time he waited he prayed and sang hymns, and he told his whole story to anyone who would listen. Then the people of Lucas loved him for his faithfulness, and they brought him hot food and warm clothes and fire. And when he told them how God let him wade across the sea they looked at him in awe, and in Eyre he was first called the Blessed.

The King heard these things, and his heart filled with hate, for Brandon had put him to shame. So he decided to kill him in secret, and crush the young fool who would dare to embarrass him.

So King Lucas called for Branwen to be brought, and he clothed her in silks and velvet once more, and he spoke to her kindly and asked her forgiveness. But none of these things did he truthfully mean, for his heart was black with anger. Branwen doubted his words, but when she heard that her brother had come at long last, her joy was so great that she forgot about the past altogether.

Then Lucas saw that his wife had forgiven him, and he knew that he owed it to Brandon. And he hated them both all the more because of that.

Then the King declared a feast to honor Queen Branwen, and all the great nobles of Eyre were invited, and even those of Cambria beyond the wide sea. For the King had a plan to be rid of

Branwen forever, and her people as well if he could.

For a month he plotted in secret, and for all that time the King gave no hint. He guarded his secret like a chest of pure gold, and only a few knew his scheme.

But on Midsummer's Day the flags were unfurled, and the feast began. On the third day the King judged the time was right, and he hid twenty soldiers behind curtains in the feast hall. The signal for attack would be the death of the Queen, when a soldier would stab her from behind. The King ordered his people that no one should disturb them or come into the feast hall, no matter what might be heard from inside. For he hoped to blame the killing on the Cambrian nobles, and give himself a reason to make war on their land.

All this was done, and the King himself stabbed the Queen, for he hated her so much that he wanted the pleasure for his own. When Branwen fell down on the cold stone floor, then the soldiers of Eyre jumped out and attacked.

The battle was fierce and long in the feast hall, but the Cambrian men were more brave than the King thought. At last no one was left except Brandon and Lucas. The rest were all dead on the floor. Then Brandon himself killed Lucas the King, and the feast hall was quiet and still.

Brandon went quickly to Branwen his sister, and he wept bitter tears, for he thought she was dead. But then he saw her still breathing, and hope filled his heart. He took care of her wound the best that he could, and then picked her up in his arms and carried her away. For he knew that the scene of the battle would be found, and then it would be death for them both if they stayed.

The people in the castle knew them both by sight, and no one dared stop them for fear of the King. They soon reached the docks on the river nearby, and Brandon took his sister to the smallest boat he could find. Then he fled from the land of King Lucas.

In three days they crossed to the Cambrian shore, and the people wept bitterly for the loss of their men, and they feared a new war would come quickly. They laid all the blame on Brandon and Branwen, and some even said they should both be killed. The mood in the town was so black at the time that Brandon knew it wasn't safe to remain there.

Therefore he and two friends took Branwen away, to a castle in the south by the shores of the sea where not many men lived. The earl of that place was a healer of hurts, and no one knew where Brandon and Branwen had gone. Therefore all the more did the townspeople curse them, as cowards who fled in the night.

But Brandon cared nothing for that, because Branwen lay close to death. At times she would open her eyes and speak, but such times grew more rare as the days passed by, and he feared she couldn't live for much longer. Then he wept in his room, and no one could comfort him.

But Brandon remembered his prayer on the beach, and how God had answered when no one else would help. So he prayed once again, and he begged that her life be spared, no matter what he might have to do to save her.

Then he saw in a vision a land which was lovely and sweet, and he saw himself walking slowly through fields of gold flowers. His hand plucked a fruit from a beautiful tree, and he saw himself give it to Branwen. Then she was healed, and the vision was over. But somehow he knew that that land was in the east.

Then Brandon arose, and he decided at once to search for that place, for he knew it was Branwen's only hope. He departed from the castle that very same day, and went down to the shore to find a ship.

But the men of that village were afraid of wild lands and uncharted seas, and at first there was no one who would help him, just as before.

At last an old man took pity, and he gave him a one-man boat barely large enough to be seaworthy. Brandon loaded it up with food for a month, for he didn't know how long he might be gone.

Then he sailed out to sea in the evening dusk, and by morning he was far from all land. For days and days he sailed to the east, alone on the ocean with little to guide him. He followed the sun, and the stars at night, till his water and food ran low. But he still went on with nothing to eat, for he knew what would happen to Branwen if he didn't.

At last he saw land not far in the distance, the first that he'd seen since leaving the castle.

Then he sailed for the shore, for he was starving and weak, and unless he found food very soon he was lost.

The minute he stepped on the beach that evening there appeared a white hound who fell at his feet. The dog barked and panted and snuffled his toes, and at last Brandon laughed at its playfulness. Then the dog jumped up and ran a short way, and looked back and waited while it wagged its long tail.

"Maybe this dog was sent here today to lead me some place I should go," Brandon thought to himself. So he followed the dog to an old wooden house, where he found a long table set full of good food. There was no one to be seen, and no one came when he called. Just the dog, who sat and watched him and licked its black lips.

So Brandon ate and drank as much as he wished, and he was thankful indeed. When he finished his food, the dog led him to a bed with the covers turned down, and there he slept until morning.

As soon as the sky turned pale he ate once again from the table, but he took nothing with him from there. The dog growled when he tried, and wouldn't allow it. So he returned to the ship, and the dog came with him, and together they followed the shore of this new land he had found.

Green pastures and meadows stretched far out of sight, and grazing on the hills were herds of white sheep. Each of those sheep was the size of a horse, and their wool was white as snow. They looked up at Brandon and bleated and stamped as he passed, the most beautiful animals that he ever saw.

At mid-afternoon he spied an old shepherd, who called to the ship and bid Brandon welcome. His hair was as white as the wool of the sheep, and Brandon went ashore to speak to him.

"This is the Island of Sheep," the man said, "and here it's never cold but always summer. So the sheep grow large and whiter than snow, because they eat the best grass that grows anywhere."

And the old man gave him food and warm clothes to take with him, and water to last him for a trip of many days, for he said that the land would soon come to an end.

So it did, and before long Brandon left the Island of Sheep behind him, and headed out again across the sea. Near the end of the day he came to a place of sharp rocks and shallow water, and he was afraid if he went on then the ship might be wrecked in the dark. But he saw a black rock that stood taller than most, and he anchored his ship beside it for the night. He ate a cold supper of dried meat and goat cheese, and next morning set out once again.

The sky was dark and cloudy when the sun rose, and Brandon had barely escaped from the sharp shallow rocks before a storm swept him up in its fury. The wind and the waves were terrible to see, and he dared not sleep for a second. It was three full days till he reached land again, so exhausted by then that he could barely hold the sail. The ship ran aground on a sand bar in the dark, and the wind and the waves howled and swirled all around him.

When the storm died away about noon the next day, then he gathered his strength to explore this new land and see what there was to see. The first thing he found was two stone wells at the edge of the woods, with the grass clipped and neat all around them. Out of one there flowed water so pure and so clear that Brandon had never seen the like of it. From the other came a stream somewhat cloudy and dark. He drank from the clear one, and it was icy cold in his mouth. Then he looked at the sand bar with a frown. The boat was aground, and he knew he was stranded, for one man alone lacked the strength to push it free.

"But if I wait just a while then the Lord will provide," he said to himself, and sat down on a rock to rest. The snow-white dog came and licked his hand, and then it lay down beside him to wait.

Before long a young man came to the well to fetch water, and he saw them both sitting there and took pity. For Brandon was dirty and salty and exhausted, and his eyes were dull from not sleeping.

The young man led him down a path to a monastery, which was hidden in the woods nearby. When they got there he was greeted by twenty-four monks, all of them clothed in scarlet and gold. The abbot sat Brandon on a hard wooden bench, and washed his sore feet with warm water. The monks washed the sea salt from his skin and his hair, and gave him clean clothes to put on. Then they took him to a place full of tables and chairs, and they all had supper together. Each monk at the table had a loaf of warm bread, and a bowl of white roots which tasted delicious, but Brandon didn't know of what kind they might be. They drank nothing but water from the first clear well. Brandon had eaten nothing for days but dried meat and cheese, and the food he got now was wonderful, he thought.

Brandon stayed with the monks for two or three days till he was rested and strong once again. Then he knew it was time to move on, for he didn't dare wait for too long. The monks worked together to push the ship off the sand, and he thanked them very deeply before leaving.

Not long after that came a huge fish that followed him, spitting streams of salty water at the ship. The water came so fast that Brandon nearly drowned, and he could barely keep the ship from sinking. But the white-furred dog didn't fear the huge fish, and he jumped in the sea with a snarl. The dog and the fish fought viciously for a while, but at last the white dog tore the fish into pieces, and swam back to sit at Brandon's side.

The next day they came to a region of darkness, where the air was full of foul smells and black smoke. Brandon heard cruel horns blasting far off in the dark, but he couldn't see a thing past the front of the boat, not even in the middle of the day. He was more afraid of this than of anything so far, but he knew in his heart there was no other way.

He sailed for hours through the smothering darkness, and he could barely even breathe for the smoke and the fumes. Then far in the distance he saw an island full of flames.

When he passed close by then a demon rushed out, and he stared at Brandon with huge bulging eyes. He turned toward the island and called to some others, the most horrible cry that could ever be imagined.

Soon there came more demons who rushed across the sea, with sharp hooks and hammers of burning iron in their hands. They ran on the water as if it were land, and it seemed like the whole sea was on fire. The things roared and snarled and threw their weapons at the ship, and they sizzled and splashed in the sea all around.

Brandon was in terror at first, and he covered his eyes from the hideous sight, but he soon found the demons couldn't hurt him. All they could do was threaten and roar, and their power came only through the terror they caused. So Brandon took courage, and pretended they didn't exist.

When the demons discovered that he no longer feared them, they gave up the ghost and went home.

Then Brandon sailed on for seven more days, and soon the darkness gave way to heavy fog mixed with sleet. The fog was so thick that he still couldn't see, not even the sun in the sky, and at last he was hopelessly lost. He couldn't even be sure which direction was home. All he could do was pray for God to lead him through, for he knew he could never find the way by himself.

Then at last the gray fog finally lifted, and Brandon could see where he was once more. The sea all around him was smooth and glassy as crystal, and not far to the east lay a silent shore.

The earth of that land shined as bright as the sun, and the stones on the ground were of diamond and pearl. Each meadow was full of gold flowers and trees, and all of the trees in that land bore fruit. The breeze brought a scent of those meadows to his ship, and tears filled his eyes and his breath nearly stopped, for nothing more beautiful could there be.

Then Brandon set foot on the bright shining beach, and before long there came to him a handsome young man, whose face shone with light.

"Be glad now, Brandon, for this is the land you've been searching for. You stand on the edge of the Land of Eden, where Adam and Eve first lived, till they broke the commandment of God. The fruit that you see is ripe all year, and the light never ceases to shine. Come in," he invited.

And Brandon smiled, and walked into Eden, and there the man left him alone. Then he wandered for a while through the meadows and woods, but he never reached the end of that land. Everything was lit in a changeless day, and it seemed to be always spring. At the last he came to a clear flowing river, but he dared not cross over, for he felt in his heart it was forbidden. Then the handsome young man came again.

"This river you see divides all things in two. On the far side there grows on the highest hill the Tree of Life in eternal bloom, and no one can cross over while he is still alive. Therefore take now a fruit from one of these other trees, and depart in peace, and sail once again to your home."

Then Brandon plucked a fruit from the tree that grew closest, and he wept as he boarded his ship once again, for he knew he could never forget that place.

He sailed to the west, and not very long afterward he reached the Cambrian shore, although he barely remembered the trip. Then the people of the castle were glad, but confused, for they said he'd been gone just three days. And Brandon could hardly believe it. Then he told them the story of his journey on the sea, and all the wonderful things that he'd seen.

"I've walked in a land that shines like the sun, and stood by the river of Eden," he told them, and no one could doubt it, for his clothes still smelled of that beautiful place.

From that day onward, wherever he went, he was called Bran the Blessed by his people, the name he was given in Eyre. For no other man walked so close with God as Brandon, whose feet had once stood in the meadows of Eden, and who had breathed for a while the clean air of that place.

The fruit which he brought from that shining land he took to his sister in her bed. And she smiled when she saw him, through the pain in her eyes.

"I knew you'd come," she whispered.

"The way was long, but now eat and be well," he told her. Then Branwen ate the fruit from his hand, and the pain slowly vanished from her eyes. She rose to her feet, whole and healthy again, and her beauty was no less than before, for sorrow and wisdom had deepened it. Then she kissed her brother and held him tight, and together they left the old castle.

The new King of Eyre was a righteous young man, and the war that was feared never came. For the tale of Bran the Blessed was repeated far and wide among the people of Eyre and Cambria, and they never grew tired of hearing it. And for love of Brandon, the people of both lands swore never to make war on each other again.

Then Bran the Blessed and Branwen the Fair lived a long life in peace, and they were honored by their people.

And in all the time since, there has never been another like Brandon. No one in all the land of Cambria has ever been so faithful and true, nor so blessed and brave as he was, and he is remembered with love even to this day.

The Land of Fear

A Tale of Wisdom

Wisdom is better than weapons of war.

- Ecclesiastes 9:18

The Land of Fear

Once there was a girl named Elisabeth, who had a most amazing adventure.

She lived in a cottage with her father and two sisters (Their names were Aline and Celeste), in the village of Brumbling, not far from the River of Fear. Now this was a terrible place where only the bravest or the most foolish people ever dared to go, for no one had ever returned.

All sorts of things were whispered about it by the people of Brumbling. Some believed that there must be a dragon, and others spoke of a terrible sorcerer in a tall black tower. A few told stories of things even more frightening. But everyone also agreed that there was a treasure so wonderful and amazing that it could not even be described.

Elisabeth had heard these things all her life long, and she burned with desire to know the real truth of the matter.

In those days a great war had come to Brumbling, and the village stood almost empty. Elisabeth was not old enough to help, and she had been left in the village with her older sisters to tend the fields and the house. Their father was an excellent bowman, and had gone away with the army for a little while. Elisabeth knew that it was necessary, but she still felt lonely without Father.

For one thing, Aline and Celeste were not very kind to her. They seemed to think that Elisabeth should do all the nasty, tedious chores that they didn't want to do, and Aline especially would pinch her unmercifully. Elisabeth endured all this until the day the town crier ran through the village, shrieking that the barbarians had defeated the army of Brumbling, and that they now demanded a mountain of gold from the people by the end of the day, or they would utterly destroy the village at sunrise tomorrow morning.

Aline and Celeste wept and screamed when they heard this news, and immediately began packing bags to run as far away as possible. Elisabeth was angry with them for being so cowardly, and told them so. But Celeste only threw a bag at her and told her not to be a fool, and Aline pinched her arm hard enough to leave bruises.

Elisabeth made up her mind that she would not run away from the barbarians with her sisters. She decided that she would herself get the mountain of gold that they demanded, by going into the forbidden lands near the River to find the treasure.

Therefore she packed the bag Celeste had given her, but instead of waiting for her sisters, she slipped quietly out the back door and ran to the barn. The hay loft was nearly full with fresh straw, and Elisabeth hid herself quite carefully in the darkest corner she could find. Aline and

Celeste never visited the barn if they could help it, for they hated to get dirty, and Celeste especially was afraid of the cows. Elisabeth herself rather liked the animals. She had spent many mornings feeding them and collecting the milk.

It wasn't long before she heard Aline calling her name, and shortly after that she heard her sister's footsteps running into the byre.

"Beth!" she called, so loud that Elisabeth could imagine her standing right under the hay loft. She kept very quiet until she heard Aline go away. That didn't take long, for she knew Aline wouldn't spend any more time looking for her than she had to.

As soon as she was sure Aline was gone, Elisabeth left the barn and walked briskly to the little creek that flowed behind her house. It was not much more than ten feet across, and she immediately began to follow it downstream, for she knew it would lead her to the river before too long. That was a good thing, for she had no wish to become lost in the woods on her way there.

Indeed it wasn't very long at all before the creek entered the edge of the forest and lost itself among the tall dark trees. Elisabeth had never been inside the forest before, for it was far too near the river for anyone's comfort, and there were the most horrifying stories told about what went on there.

One of these stories in particular was on Elisabeth's mind as she looked at the opening. Her Tante Cheri had told her, long ago, that there were ghouls that haunted the woods, hideous beasts wrapped in rotting grave clothes who waited with dripping mouths to kill and eat anyone who ventured into the darkness under the trees. Elisabeth had pretended not to be scared at the time, but now she couldn't help wondering if there might not really be something in there after all. The woods looked very dark and scary.

However, while she hesitated at the edge, she suddenly heard the very last thing she wanted to hear.

"Beth!" came Celeste's voice, somewhere not too far behind her. Elisabeth made up her mind quickly. Without even looking back to see how close Celeste might be, she took off running toward the woods as fast as she could go. She could move very quickly when she wanted to, and it was no more than a few seconds before she felt the trees close in around her. She didn't stop even then, but continued running along the creek bank until the edge of the woods was far behind her. Celeste would never follow her among the trees, of that she was certain. She hadn't forgotten about the ghouls, but she determined to go ahead anyway.

The creek gurgled and bubbled placidly along beside her while she walked, and after a few hours (during which she saw no ghouls at all), Elisabeth came abruptly to the bank of the river. The creek flowed out past a little cottonwood tree and lost itself in the main current, so that she now had no path to follow.

There was a sort of beach at the place where she stood, of rocks and sand. The river was nothing special, as far as Elisabeth could tell. There was certainly nothing scary or unusual about it. Since she had come back out into the daylight, the whole idea of ghouls and magic had begun to seem rather silly again. She looked up and down the bank without seeing anything to give her a goal to move toward, so she sat down on the warm sand to think about it a while.

Elisabeth had often gone down to the creek to play in the sand or skip rocks on the water if she could find any good ones, and she began absentmindedly tossing pebbles into the river while she thought about what to do. The current must have been swift, for it snatched away the ripples almost as soon as they formed. She hadn't been doing this for very long when a huge silver fish came to the top of the water and looked at her.

"I do wish you would quit dropping rocks into my bedroom," the fish growled, in a bubbly, fishy sort of voice.

"I'm sorry. . . I didn't know you were there," Elisabeth said, too startled to think of anything else to say.

"What?! You didn't know that fishes live in the river?" the fish demanded, insulted.

"No. . . I mean yes, I did know that; I just never thought about it before," Elisabeth admitted.

"Humph," the fish grumbled, "Well, I forgive you just this once, since you're only a girl and couldn't possibly be expected to know any better, but it had best not happen ever again."

Now Elisabeth thought the fish was being very rude, and she stood up to tell him so, but just as she reached the edge of the water she twisted her ankle on a loose stone and fell down. It hurt fairly badly, and she began to rub it.

"Tsk, tsk. . . clumsy as well as stupid," the fish commented, watching her. Elisabeth lost her patience, for she disliked rude and insensitive people.

"You could at least ask if I was alright. I might have broken my ankle, you know," she told him disapprovingly.

"But you didn't, now did you?" he asked her cheerfully, as if that solved the whole matter. She was still trying to think how to reply to such a question when the fish went on without waiting for her answer.

"Still, you might have an idea. That could be a nasty bruise later on. I'd better get you something for it," he said, almost to himself. Before she could reply, he disappeared under the water again.

The fish wasn't actually gone very long, but Elisabeth did have time to stand up and put some weight on her ankle. The pain was too much to bear, and it forced her to sit down again. Before long the fish reappeared, holding a thin sliver of what looked like beaver wood in its mouth. He spit it out on the beach, then coughed up a bit of mucus and blew it into the water. Elisabeth looked at him with disgust.

"Well, are you going to pick up the stick, or what?" the fish asked her impatiently. Truthfully, Elisabeth would rather have had nothing else to do with the fish, but she decided that if he meant to help her she ought to be polite. She reached out and picked up the beaver stick. It was still slimy from the fish's mouth and from whatever nasty place it had been taken from. She held it with distaste.

"Well, aren't you going to use it?" the fish demanded.

"What's it for, and how am I supposed to use it?" she asked, getting annoyed herself now.

"I would have thought even a little girl would know what to do with *that*," the fish told her. She could almost imagine him rolling his eyes at her. . . if he had had any eyelids.

"But never mind. Touch the stick to your ankle," he told her. Elisabeth did so, and instantly the pain disappeared. She stood up carefully to test it out, and to her surprise she found that her ankle was completely well again. She looked up at the fish.

"Thank you," she told him, and meant it.

"Well. . . I couldn't have a litterbug lolling around on my doorstep all day," the fish muttered. Elisabeth was willing to tolerate his gruffness now, so she let it pass. She started to hand him back the stick.

"No, no. . . you keep it, missie. I don't need it anymore," he grumbled. Elisabeth slipped the stick into her pocket and fastened the button, and while she was thinking about what else to say to the fish, he suddenly disappeared back into the river, without so much as a flick of his tail to say goodbye.

"Well, Mr. Fish, I'll certainly remember not to throw any more rocks into your bedroom," she said to herself, looking at the spot where the fish had disappeared. A few bubbles were coming up from somewhere below, but she couldn't tell if he heard her or not.

After a while, Elisabeth realized she couldn't stand on the bank all day. She had to find some way to keep going. Upstream was a thicket of bamboo, which looked so tangled and heavy that she doubted she could ever get through it. Behind her was the ghoul-haunted forest, and she was still uneasy about going back in there. Ahead of her was the river, much too wide and strong to think of swimming.

"And so," she said to herself, "that really leaves only one way left. Downstream it is." In that direction the rocky beach went on for quite some time, and Elisabeth followed it. Now and then she had to stop and dump sand and pebbles out of her shoes, but otherwise the going was not too difficult.

Eventually, though, she came to a knot of wild thorn trees that completely blocked the way. Elisabeth was not anxious to go in among the thorn trees, because they were wickedly sharp. The river looked a bit shallower near the edge, and she decided after much thought to try wading in the shallows until she got past the thorn thicket. Then maybe she could continue on her way.

She took off her shoes and held them so they wouldn't get wet, and then gingerly stepped into the water. It was warm as summer, not freezing cold as she had half expected it would be.

The bottom seemed to be mostly gravel in that place, which made it easy to keep her footing.

Not quite easy enough, though. She had made it most of the way around the thorn thicket when she lost her balance and fell into the deep water with a huge splash. The current snatched her at once, and almost before she knew what was happening it had carried her far from the shore. She lost her shoes and tried her best to swim toward the bank, but the swirling river was too strong, and she was getting farther away from land every second.

Elisabeth began to get frightened, and that is always a very bad thing to do when one is swimming. But before she could get really terrified, she felt her feet drag the bottom for just a second, and she turned her head to see an island right behind her.

Elisabeth wasted no time forgetting about the distant shore. She could reach the island, and that was all she cared about. She grabbed a muddy root that hung out into the water and hung on for dear life. The current tried to tear her away, but gradually she was able to pull herself along the root until she reached the shore. She climbed up out of the water, soaking wet and shivering in the light breeze.

The island wasn't very big. In fact, it was barely more than a sand bar with a few tough bushes growing on it. Elisabeth looked out across the river and immediately gave up all hope of swimming back to the bank she'd just come from. It was much too far, and the river was too swift.

She crossed the island and found that it wasn't nearly so far to the bank on that side. Only about a hundred feet of sluggish backwater separated the island from solid ground. But that way was choked with fallen logs and brush that didn't look appealing at all. Elisabeth knew she couldn't stay on the island forever, but how was she to get off?

She was staring at the log jam, wondering if she might possibly risk walking across it, when she got a nasty surprise.

"Hello, miss. Can I help you?" a cheerful voice asked her. Elisabeth was startled, and looked down at her feet to see an alligator floating in the water. He was much too close to her feet for comfort, and Elisabeth stepped back hastily. The alligator giggled. Not a deep laugh like you might have expected, but a high-pitched giggle that reminded Elisabeth of her sisters in one of their silliest moods.

"Surely you're not afraid, are you?" it asked her, and giggled again.

"Um... just a little bit," Elisabeth admitted, for she was a very truthful girl. The alligator stopped giggling to itself and looked at her for a long time.

"Hmm. . . . no, I don't think you'd make more than a mouthful, so you need not be afraid," it told her. Elisabeth didn't like that answer much, but she thought it was best not to argue. The alligator might change its mind.

"I need to get across the river," she told him, changing the subject.

"I'd be glad to give you a lift over the water," the alligator said brightly, with a toothy smile that didn't do anything at all to make Elisabeth feel better. While she hesitated, the alligator went on without waiting for an answer.

"What are you doing here by the river, anyway? We don't often get human beings down this way," he said.

"An army of barbarians has invaded my village, and they want a mountain of gold or they'll destroy everything. So I came here to find it," she told him.

"Hmm. . . well now that's not very nice of them, is it? No, not nice at all," the gator giggled.

"It's not really very funny," Elisabeth scolded him.

"Ah, no, no, I suppose it isn't," the gator agreed, still smirking. Elisabeth was about to decide the alligator was just as annoying as the fish had been, if that was possible. But the fish had helped her, and maybe the alligator could help her too.

"Do you know where I could find any gold?" she asked him hopefully.

"Ah, gold! No, there's no gold anywhere near the river. We have no use for that sort of thing," he declared. Elisabeth was crushed, for it seemed that her trip to the river was a huge waste of time after all, and tears began to fall from her eyes into the water.

"Ah, missie, you mustn't cry now," the alligator told her hastily. Elisabeth lost her patience.

"The barbarians will destroy my village if they don't get that gold. Why shouldn't I cry about that?" she demanded hotly. The gator seemed taken aback for a moment, but he soon regained his composure. He giggled again, which irritated Elisabeth to no end.

"Well now, I might be able to tell you something useful about that, I might. I just might," he said, smiling mysteriously. He was obviously enjoying himself very much. Elisabeth stopped crying and waited for him to tell her what it was, but he didn't say a word.

"What was it you could tell me?" she finally asked, when the silence had stretched out for a minute or more.

"I thought you'd never ask!" the gator exclaimed, with another attack of giggles.

"It's true there's no gold in this place, but there's something much better," he whispered. Elisabeth was interested now and leaned close to hear better.

"What is it?" she asked.

"On the far bank of the river, a little downstream, there's a ruined stone tower. And in a room at the top of that tower there lives a huge snowy owl. And if you bring him something he likes well enough, he can grant you a wish. Anything you want. Even a mountain of gold," the gator informed her. Elisabeth was overjoyed at that news, and her face lit up. The gator saw it.

"Ah, not so fast, missie! If you go to the owl emptyhanded, or if you bring him something he doesn't like, then he'll eat you for supper instead of giving you a wish," the alligator warned her. That did put a crimp in things, Elisabeth had to admit. She wasn't ready to give up yet, though.

"What does the owl like?" she asked.

"No one has ever figured that out. Only one man ever came back out of the tower alive, and he isn't talking," the gator told her, nodding mysteriously again.

"Where can I find that man? Why won't he talk to anybody?" she demanded.

"Because, when he came out from visiting the owl he tried to cross the river, and I ate him up," the gator told her with another one of those toothy smiles. Elisabeth stepped back from the shore in sudden alarm. The gator slipped into another attack of giggles, so much so that he choked on a mouthful of water and had to cough.

"Just pulling your leg, missie," he told her, when he was able to contain himself.

"That wasn't funny," she scowled.

"Ah, but it was! But truly, I'll be glad to give you a ride across the water on my back, if you like," he offered again.

Elisabeth honestly didn't like that idea at all, but she couldn't think of any other way to get off the island. She had to get to the owl. As soon as she figured out what would keep him from eating her for supper, that was. So she gathered her courage and climbed on the alligator's back. He faithfully carried her across the river as he said he would, and deposited her on the shore. She was glad to be on solid ground again.

"Just follow the river downstream, and you'll come to the tower before long!" he called out as he swam away, and giggled again. Elisabeth watched him until he disappeared, and then set off down the bank. Walking barefoot slowed her down considerably, and she wished she hadn't lost her shoes.

Even so, it wasn't very long before she saw a black stone tower rising above the trees near the bank, just as the alligator had said she would.

There she stopped, because she had no idea what the owl might like. What could she give him that he didn't already have?

It was also still daylight, and she remembered that owls liked to sleep during the day. She certainly didn't want to annoy him by waking him up early. So in the meantime she sat down on a dead log to wait.

By the time it started to get dark she still hadn't thought of any good answer to the question of what to give the owl, and she was afraid he would soon leave the tower to go hunting for the night. Elisabeth knew there wasn't time to wait and think about it any longer. The barbarians would destroy Brumbling at sunrise if they didn't have the gold by then.

She therefore decided to go in and speak to the owl boldly, and try to make a deal with him. She hadn't forgotten what the alligator said about being eaten for supper, but that was a risk she decided she'd just have to take.

She approached the tower slowly, not eager at all to face the owl any sooner than she had to. There was a door in the base of the tower which seemed to be the only way in, and at first she was afraid it would be locked. But when she touched it, she soon discovered that it was made of wood so rotten that she could pull it apart with her bare hands. She tore down enough of the door to squeeze through, and found herself in an open room that took up the entire bottom floor of the tower. There was a stone staircase that circled the outer wall and led up through the ceiling, and she knew that had to be where the owl lived. She took a deep breath to calm her fear and then very resolutely climbed up to meet him.

There were three floors to the tower, and when she reached the top one, Elisabeth found the owl. He was sitting on a nest made of branches and straw, looking out into the gathering dusk through a big ragged hole in the stone wall. He was white as snow, and he had to have been at least the size of a horse. His eyes were big as dinner plates, and his beak looked sharper than a knife, with a cruel hook on the end. He must have heard her coming up the stairs, for he turned to look at her when she came in.

"Why have you come here?" he asked, getting right to the point. For a moment Elisabeth was too terrified to speak, but at last she found her voice.

"Sir Owl, I'm sorry to disturb you. But an army has attacked my village, and they will destroy it this very sunrise unless we give them a mountain of gold. I came here because I was told that you could do this, if I wished it," she said, in a voice that she hoped sounded braver than she felt. The owl studied her with its dinner-plate eyes for a while.

"Not many are brave enough to come here and ask, but yes, I could do that. But surely you know the price. What have you brought me?" he said at last. This was the moment Elisabeth had been dreading.

"Sir Owl, I had no idea what you might wish for, but if there's anything I have or can get for you, I will do it," she told him. The owl looked impatient.

"Now don't tell me you're one of *those* kind," he said in disgust. Then he seemed to think better of it.

"As a matter of fact there *is* something I want, but you could never get it for me. It lies at the bottom of the river, and the current is very deep and strong. Since you came here for someone else's sake and not for greed, I'll let you go without eating you tonight, but don't bother me again," the owl told her, and then turned as if to go. Elisabeth couldn't let her only chance slip away.

"Sir Owl, what is this thing you want? I promise I'll find a way to get it for you!" she cried. The owl looked back at her in annoyance.

"Still here? I thought I told you to go away before I eat you," he growled.

"I have to know what will save my village," she told him, not backing down.

"You're a plucky one," he commented, half to himself. "Alright, then, girl. If you're so sure of yourself then I'll tell you what I want, and if you can bring it here before the night is over then I'll grant your wish. But if not, then I'll find you and eat you for breakfast, no matter where you may try to hide. Will you make that deal?" he demanded.

"Yes sir," she told him without hesitation. He looked amazed, but he didn't try to talk her out of it anymore. He simply began to tell her what she needed to know.

"Long ago, I had a magical piece of wood that kept me young and strong at all times, and it could heal any sickness or injury there was. But as I flew across the river one night, another owl attacked me by surprise. He thought he could kill me and take my tower and my magic. How the feathers flew in the moonlight! I ate him for supper that night. But during the fight I dropped my stick in the river, and without it I'll soon grow old and weak, and then another owl will take my place after all. But no one can dredge it up from the bottom of the river, even if it hasn't been washed down to the sea. You won't be able to do it either, but maybe you'll taste better than a deer or a goat in the morning," the owl said.

Elisabeth shivered, but she reached in the pocket of her dress, thankful indeed for the button that held it shut.

"Is this what you want, Sir Owl?" she asked, pulling out the stick she'd gotten from the fish. The owl gasped when he saw it, which sounded very strange.

"Where did you find that? Give it to me at once!" he cried. Elisabeth held out the stick so the owl could grasp it in one of his razor-sharp talons.

He snatched it from her as fast as he could get close enough, as if afraid she might change her mind. When he managed to contain his pleasure, he looked at her again.

"Well! You lived up to your end of the bargain, so now I must live up to mine. You get just one wish, missie, so take care! Use it wisely," he told her.

"Then I wish for a mountain of-" she began, but the owl interrupted her.

"I'll offer you a bit of advice, missie, and if you're wise then you'll take it. Don't ask for that mountain of gold, because if you do then who's to say the barbarians will keep their word? They may take the gold and destroy the village anyway. And even if they don't, then another enemy may appear someday, or another disaster may come. Think of more than just today," he urged her. Elisabeth saw that this was good advice, but it left her wondering what she should ask for.

"What should I wish for then?" she finally asked the owl.

"Hoo. . . no one has ever asked me that before," he told her, seeming surprised.

"But I need to know," she insisted.

"Then ask for wisdom, missie. Because wisdom is the chief thing, and if you have that, then everything else will fall into place," he told her. It seemed just like the sort of thing an owl would say.

"Then I wish to be the wisest person in the world," she said. The owl couldn't smile with his beak, but Elisabeth was certain she could hear it in his voice when he spoke.

"Your wish is granted. And because you trusted me and asked for the best thing of all, I will destroy your enemies myself," he told her.

And it was so. Elisabeth made her way back to Brumbling with no further adventures the next day, and she found that all the barbarians had been destroyed or driven away during the night, just as the owl had promised her.

No one thought to ask where Elisabeth had been. No one except Celeste, that is, who had seen her go into the forest. But when Celeste pressed her to know what she had seen and done, Elisabeth would only smile and say nothing.

Thus it was that no one in Brumbling ever knew that Elisabeth had saved them from the barbarians at the risk of her life, and she was content to have it so. But in later years, her wisdom was such that the people often came to her for help with their most difficult problems, and they were often amazed at the words that came from her mouth.

In time, her fame spread even to other villages, so that there were always visitors at the little cottage who wished to speak with her. Many of the visitors were wealthy and important people, and left rich gifts at her feet. And at last she was held in such awe by the people of many lands that no one would have dreamed of attacking Brumbling ever again. Thus it happened even as the owl had told her it would; by asking for wisdom, she had received wealth and honor and power as well, without even needing to ask.

And Elisabeth lived a long and happy life in blessedness.

Jacob Have I Loved

A Tale of Grace

Can a mother forget the babe at her breast, and have no compassion on the son she has borne? Although she may forget, yet I will not forget you. . .

- Isaiah 49:15

Jacob Have I Loved

Jacob found the amulet in an old cigar box in the attic. He wasn't looking for it, or anything in particular really. He just liked rooting around up there sometimes. Especially on days when he didn't want Mama to find him, and that was more often than not.

She had a hangover today, like she did most Saturday mornings, and that always put her in a bad mood. She wasn't above smacking your face on days like that, so Jacob had decided it was best to disappear for a while. Out of sight, out of mind.

It had been raining when he woke up this morning, so that meant he couldn't leave the house. His brother Joey was still asleep with his thumb in his mouth, and Jacob had kissed him and tucked him in a little tighter before he tiptoed across the creaky hardwood floor and pulled an old red t-shirt over his head. Mama had kept both of them awake till almost two o'clock this morning before she finally passed out on the couch, and little ones needed their sleep. Joey was four... not quite twelve years younger than his big brother, and Jacob loved him more than anything in the world.

Jacob had never been able to go back to sleep right after he woke up in the morning. So he came up to the attic instead, where he could sit among Papaw's old stuff and daydream a while. No matter how much he looked, there was always something new to see.

This morning, he was digging through an old army trunk which was full of assorted junk, mostly trinkets and souvenirs Papaw had brought back from Germany. Most of them were tossed in the trunk carelessly, with no particular order. Jacob picked up anything that looked interesting, played with it for a few minutes, and then put it back. Once in a while he found something he especially liked, and these things he sometimes set aside to take downstairs.

He found the cigar box in the bottom of the trunk under a piece of cardboard, almost like someone had tried to hide it down there. That made him curious, so he pulled it out and blew dust off the lid, and tore off an old strip of duct tape that held it closed. Inside he found some crumpled rice paper yellowed with age, and wrapped up inside it was a silver necklace with a small medallion-type amulet attached. It was badly tarnished in spite of the wrapping, but there was no doubt what it was.

Jacob was delighted. Real treasure!

There were seven blue gems set in a circle on the front of the medallion, but nothing else special about it that he could see. He turned it over in his hands, discovering an inscription on the back which he couldn't make out through the tarnish. He spit on the edge of his shirt tail and rubbed hard until he could read it, but even then he was none the wiser. The amulet simply said "Thumb here." The letters were sloppy and blocky, like someone had scratched them there with the point of a pocket knife.

"Thumb here?" he repeated aloud, thinking to himself what a strange thing that was for someone to put on a piece of jewelry. It was clear enough, though, so he shrugged his shoulders and stuck his thumb where it said, thinking how much nicer the amulet would look if it wasn't covered with tarnish.

"Ow!" he cried wildly as a sharp pain stabbed his hand. It felt like he was touching a hot coal, and he dropped the amulet instinctively. He looked at his thumb and saw no visible cut or scratch. It didn't hurt anymore either, and his alarm changed quickly to puzzlement. He flexed his hand, and it moved smoothly. Nothing seemed to be hurt. He listened to see if anybody was coming to check on him, but the house was silent. Apparently he hadn't been as loud as he thought.

He stared down at the amulet suspiciously, and then cautiously prodded it with his big toe.

Nothing happened, but he noticed that the black tarnish was gone. Silver gleamed brightly even in the weak light from the louvered window. Eventually he got bold enough to pick it up by the chain and look more closely. A ring of tiny words was now etched sharply into the gleaming surface around the edge of the medallion, but they looked like nothing Jacob had ever seen before. Whatever language they were, he couldn't understand them.

That clumsy "thumb here" was still scratched into the surface on the back, and he could read that part just fine, but Jacob had no intention of following *that* advice again. No thanks!

He had no idea what had happened, or how the tarnish had suddenly disappeared, or what it was that hurt his finger. But he was determined to find out. He liked mysteries, and this was an especially interesting one. So he thought back carefully, trying to remember every detail of the experience to see if there were any clues.

Well, he'd been thinking the amulet would look nice if it was clean, and now there it was, just like he imagined it would be, with no polishing or anything. He started to feel a tinge of excitement. Jacob had always believed there had to be something more out there than just the dull and humdrum world he was used to. So when something magical was suddenly dropped in his lap, he wasn't at all disbelieving, as some people might have been. When reality is harsh, you learn very quickly to look beyond it.

He soon decided it was worth hurting his thumb again, if that's what it took to find out the truth. He looked at his shirt tail, where the spit-and-tarnish mixture from earlier was gradually turning into a smudged brown stain, and decided that would make as good an experiment as any. Therefore he took the amulet in hand, and cautiously touched his thumb to the back. There was no pain this time.

"I wish my shirt was clean," he said distinctly. His head was full of vague ideas from a hundred fairy tales and movies about how things like this were supposed to work, but in this case he was disappointed. Nothing happened. Jacob wasn't willing to give up yet, though. He looked down at an old pair of socks on the floor.

"Come here," he ordered them in a firm tone.   Again nothing happened, and Jacob was frustrated. What was he not doing right?

He tried to recall again what he'd been doing when the tarnish disappeared. He'd been looking at the amulet, thinking about how it would look if it was clean. He hadn't actually said a word, come to think of it. He'd just thought it. Okay then, so maybe he had to visualize what he wanted, instead of talking out loud. He decided to try it again.

This time he didn't say anything, just envisioned the socks rising up off the floor and landing beside him on top of the trunk. Now there was no doubt about it. The socks floated obligingly off the floor and came to rest beside his elbow, exactly where he'd wanted them to go. There was still no more pain though, and Jacob broke into a grin.

"Yes!" he said to himself, jumping up with so much enthusiasm that he almost knocked his head against a rafter. He lost interest in exploring the attic anymore that day. He had something much more exciting than that now.

He opened the heavy attic door without a peep and crept stealthily down the uncarpeted stairs, stepping lightly and near the edges to avoid creaks. A thin film of dusty grime had sifted out of the wallboards since the last time he swept, and tiny particles of dust clung unpleasantly to the bottom of his bare feet every time he took a step. He made a face and wished for the millionth time that it wasn't so hard to keep the place clean.

The kitchen was deserted when he got to the bottom of the stairs, and he surveyed the wreckage from last night glumly. Glasses half full of unfinished milk from supper stood huddled together on the dull green Formica countertop, and dirty plates were piled high in the sink. An empty vodka bottle lay at a drunken angle against the base of the refrigerator where Mama had thrown it, and a fleet of sodden cigarette butts floated grotesquely in a pool of spilled beer on the floor. A slightly dried-out meatball lay in solitary splendor under Joey's chair on a thin veneer of splattered spaghetti sauce.

There was more, but Jacob had seen enough. The cleanup job would be bad enough without having to think about it ahead of time.

Unless. . .

He started to reach for the amulet, and then thought better of it. It wouldn't do for Mama to find out about it. He could hear her in the bathroom, putting her makeup on. Something clattered on the floor and he heard a curse. It sounded like she was in an especially nasty mood, and he felt a strong urge to disappear again. For a second, up in the attic, he'd completely forgotten about his mother, and that was always a serious mistake.

He glanced outside. The rain had stopped for now, and there was nothing to keep him from leaving the house for a while if he wanted to. He had a mind to go out in the woods and see what the amulet could do, in a place where he wouldn't be disturbed. He was eager to find out. But he hesitated, thinking about Joey. He'd most likely sleep till noon after being up so late last night, but then again he might not, and he was usually cranky when he first woke up. Mama didn't handle things like that very well. But on the other hand, Jacob didn't relish the idea of taking Joey with him and letting him find out about the amulet either. It was impossible for him to keep a secret unless he immediately forgot about it, and this was something Jacob definitely didn't want anybody to know about. Mama would take the amulet away from him before he even got a chance to do anything with it, if she knew.

The horrible idea of Mama getting the amulet was enough to settle it. There was no way Jacob was letting *that* happen. He decided Joey would be alright, and tiptoed quietly across the faded yellow linoleum to the back door. As an afterthought he paused to grab a chunk of stale cornbread from the pan on top of the stove. It was two days old, but he was hungry, and he wasn't that fussy about breakfast.

He shut the screen door slowly behind him, careful not to let the rusty hinges squeak too loud. It didn't seem to matter how often he oiled them, that high-pitched squeal always came back in a few days. He listened to make sure the house was still quiet, and then set off purposefully across the pasture.

The grass was still soaked with cold rain, making him shiver when his feet sunk in. The water washed off all the grime from the house, turning his toes a bright pink from the chill.

He finished wolfing down the cornbread before he reached the spot on the far side of the pasture that he was aiming for. The bottom strand of barbed wire had rusted in two at that point, making it easy to crawl under the loose middle strand without much trouble, at least when the ground was dry. He and Joey had done it lots of times, and their feet had scuffed a wide track of bare ground. Today there was a shallow mudhole full of red clay that oozed up between his toes like jelly.

He didn't feel like getting muddy that morning, so instead he pushed down the middle strand and gingerly climbed through the narrow slot between it and the top wire. Carelessness led to ripped clothes, and that was the last thing Jacob wanted. He was hoping to get a new pair of jeans and a shirt or two before school started, but he knew it wasn't a sure thing. Mama's finances were as changeable as her moods, and there was no telling what shape either one of them would be in from day to day. That's why it was best to be careful with what you already had.

The piney woods beyond the fence were morning silent. Every footstep crunched wetly on dead vines and pine straw, and Jacob could hear the faint sound of the sawmill planer two miles away.

Muddy pools of water popped up all around him as he got close to the creek, but Jacob paid no mind to that. He knew the path, and even when he had to wade through the spots where it was flooded, he wasn't deterred. By and by the trail curved away northward, following the little valley up into the mountains, and before long he came to higher and drier ground again.

At one place, an outcrop of stone jutted out over the creek, with a beautiful view of almost the whole valley to the south and a deep swimming hole underneath where you could cannonball off the rock if you were brave enough, and beyond it there was the wooded mountainside where no one ever went. That's where Jacob was headed.

He and Joey had named that place Black Rock, though Jacob couldn't really remember why. It didn't really look black, except when it was wet. It was Joey's favorite spot when the weather was nice, because there were lots of lizards and bugs to catch while they basked in the sun, and there was a sandy beach beside the creek that was perfect for castle building. Jacob liked to go there and read or throw rocks even when Joey wasn't with him, because it was a good place to be alone with his thoughts. But today he had other things in mind.

A low growl of thunder rolled through the heavy pine woods, reminding him that the rain might not be over quite yet. It sounded like it was only a matter of time before he got drenched, and he started to wonder if maybe it wasn't such a good idea to leave the house after all.

He hesitated, torn between wanting to find out about the amulet and not wanting to get soaked. Eventually curiosity turned out to be stronger though, so he continued on his way. If it started to rain too bad, he could always stand under a tree. It wasn't quite ten minutes later when he finally stood on top of the big stone outcrop.

The castle he and Joey had built last week on the sand bar had melted into a shapeless blob coated with pockmarks from the rain, and there were deer tracks coming down to the water to drink. Little bits of embedded mica twinkled on the surface of the Rock, which was still dark and wet in most places.

Jacob pulled the amulet out of his pocket and toyed with it. The jewelled silver glittered like broken glass, even on a cloudy day. The chain slipped through his fingers like ice, not picking up the slightest bit of dirt from his muddy hands. It was a beautiful piece of work, whoever made it. Strangely enough, there was no clasp or catch on it as you would have expected to find on a necklace. The chain was made all in one continuous piece. The only way to put it on was to slip it over your head.

Jacob hesitated before doing that. He wasn't on good terms with pain in any form, and he still remembered what had happened to his thumb earlier. It had only happened that once, to be sure, but what if the same thing happened to his neck or chest? He wasn't keen to find out. But an amulet is meant to be worn, and there was so much he needed to know. . . With a deep breath, he whisked the chain over his head before he could change his mind.

It hung lightly around his neck, the silver disk laying flat against his heart. He grasped it in his hand and held it as far away from his body as he could before he tried anything else with it. Might as well be as careful as possible.

He was coated with mud and dirt from the flooded bottoms, and he could feel scattered smudges of thick red clay slowly pulling hair as they dried on bare skin. His face was slick with oily sweat, curling down in streamers from his forehead. This gave him an idea for his first experiment.

"I wish I was clean," he said, imagining himself just that way. Again he felt nothing at all, but when he looked down every particle of dirt had vanished from his body. His clothes were cool and fresh, and even his teeth felt newly brushed. Jacob smiled with pleasure, more confident now. His eye fell on a nearby rock.

"Come here," he commanded it, holding out his right hand. The rock trembled and then gracefully floated into his outstretched hand. Jacob laughed with delight, throwing the rock into the creek and running farther up the path into the woods, looking for more things to work his magic on. He'd always been afraid to go very far that way because Mama had told him there were bears, but today he felt ready to fight bare-handed with a mountain lion. He was a force to be reckoned with now, and he silently dared anything to attack him.

It was much drier the higher he went, and the mixed pine woods slowly gave way to stands of hickory and white oak. The path wandered for miles up and over Jack Mountain, and Jacob wasn't sure where it finally came out. Now and then he kicked rocks off the path, and a few times sent them flying over the treetops with a flourish of his amulet. Nothing could have knocked a chip off his delight or erased one single particle of his satisfaction. He played with the amulet fondly, dreaming such dreams as would have seemed unbelievable just yesterday. But now! Now all things were possible.

He abruptly came out into a little meadow where the path petered out, and there he paused to catch his breath. The summer sun had scorched the tall grass into a wide field of standing hay, which not even the recent rains had been able to bring back to life. The dirt was pale and rocky, full of little white stones that looked like the bleaching skulls of field mice. This was as far as Jacob had ever been before. He knew the path picked up again somewhere on the other side, but he decided that could wait for another day when the weather was nicer. Late summer was always either hot and dry or else muggy as a wet glove, and Jacob didn't like either one.

A wild thought entered his mind, and he began to smile at the very audacity of it. His feet carried him slowly to the center of the little meadow and his left hand reached up to clasp the amulet curiously. Could he do it?

"Give me spring," he whispered, conjuring up the vivid image in his mind. Before the last word fell from his lips, the meadow began to change before his eyes. The dry grass broke up into wispy fragments quickly swept away by the wind. Dormant seeds burst into new life in a spreading pool of green around his feet, sending up pale green tendrils already heavy with the buds of flowers. Lavender stars peppered the ground with a sprinkle of blooms, and chains of golden daffodils appeared across the far side of the meadow.

For a second he was awed, and stood staring at the changes he'd made. He thought about gathering up armfuls of the daffodils and carrying them back home to brighten up the drab old house just a little. Mama liked flowers, although she might. . . well, what would she do, actually? When he stopped to think about it, he realized he was dreaming with his head in the sand. Mama wasn't a fool. She knew it wasn't the right time of year for daffodils, and at the very least she'd wonder where he got them. And then what would he say?

It wasn't just the daffodils, of course. Anything strange that happened around the house might cause problems. Mama was paranoid, and he knew from experience that it didn't take much to set her off. The least careless remark, the most minor incident; any of those things could cause an explosion.

It came to mind again that Joey would probably be the worst problem he had when it came to keeping the secret. He was seldom out of Jacob's company, and he was way too curious about things. He also couldn't keep his mouth shut to save his life. He just didn't understand the need.

The cool wind had dried a sweaty trail of hair against the curve of his cheek, and Jacob absentmindedly brushed it away. He turned his back on Spring, having temporarily lost his taste for any more playing around. He unraveled a sprig of honeysuckle from his ankle and headed back for the downward path, feeling deflated. What good was magic if you couldn't use it?

He walked quietly into the leaf-scented shade of the hickory trees, paying no attention to anything above the tips of his toes. He was lost too deep in thought. He decided it was probably about time he headed home. Joey would be waking up soon, and he didn't like the thought of leaving him alone with Mama for too long. It wasn't safe.

There was one more thing to do before he went home, though.

When he got to the Rock, Jacob went to a gnarled oak tree that leaned dangerously far out over the creek; his well trusted hiding place. The water was licking hungrily at the handful of roots it still had, and one of these days it would fall over. Maybe today, if the rain kept on much longer. Jacob slipped his hand inside the highest knothole he could reach, and pulled out an old Crown Royal bag, listening to the coins jingle inside. Jacob liked Crown Royal bags. The purple cloth and gold trim made him feel rich, like a king.

Feeling rich and being rich were two different things, of course. Jacob's hoard contained exactly eighteen dollars and sixteen cents, painstakingly collected over the past two months. Quarters left over from trips to the store, nickels and dimes salvaged from sidewalks and baseboards, all of it had gone into his hiding place. Jacob had learned to be tight as treebark with his money, but sometimes there were things he didn't mind spending it on, and now was one of those times. It was Joey's birthday next week.

Jacob stuffed the bag in his pocket, and he felt a fat raindrop land on his arm just as he turned to go. He looked up at the sky uneasily. Dark clouds were piled up like play-doh in the west, and the wind was starting to pick up again. From where he stood, he could see rain falling from the clouds in gray sheets maybe half a mile away, and it was moving his direction.

He made a run for it, gambling on the chance he could make it to the house before the rain did. Jacob was a fast runner, and if he'd been wearing his shoes he might possibly have made it in time.

He was barefoot, though, and that slowed him down just a bit. He was crawling through the fence when the rain caught him, causing him to tear a long rip in his t-shirt and leave a bloody scratch on his back. He cussed under his breath and ran across the pasture to the back door. He wasn't quite soaking wet, but close enough not to make much difference.

He scuffed his feet and made sure to let the screen door slam when he walked into the kitchen. If he made a little noise he could let Mama know he was back without actually having to speak to her. He noticed the back of her head where she sat on the couch watching one of her soaps. On the screen, an actress was passionately kissing a character Jacob had never seen before, and Mama seemed rapt. She either didn't notice him or didn't bother to say anything. Jacob didn't really care which.

He didn't see Joey with her, so he slipped upstairs as quickly and quietly as possible. Another quick touch of his amulet wiped out the creak in the seventh step just as his foot touched it, and a third swept the dust from them all. He thought about mending some of the cracks in the wallpaper but soon decided that would be too obvious. Caution, caution was the thing to remember. He could always say he'd fixed the step if anyone noticed, but the wallpaper couldn't be handled like that.

Jacob was a little curious when he found no Joey in their room either, but the mystery didn't concern him that much yet. He sat in his rocking chair by the window, daydreaming about all the great things he would do. He was still wet from the rain, so he used the amulet to dry off. The metal had picked up his body heat and lay almost unnoticed against his skin, just a round flattened lump under his t-shirt.

He traced the shape with his forefinger, caressing it and fiddling with the chain. The first shock of disappointment at having to keep things secret had begun to wear off now, and he was in the mood to play some more, if he could keep things quiet. Mama was wrapped up in her soaps, and with Joey gone it seemed like a good time to try something. But what to do?

A tiny fleck of paint on one of the windowpanes caught his eye, and with a snap of his fingers it was gone. The windowsill was already as clean as he could scrub it, but upon further inspection he decided it still lacked something. He erased the paint off the surface and polished the wood underneath so that it almost glowed. Jacob contemplated this change for a second, then dyed the faded curtains a rich midnight blue, at the same time mending every tiny run and spot-hole.

The colorful window was in such contrast to the rest of the room that Jacob decided to try some other things, just to see how it would look. He could always put it back the way it was.

He turned his attention to the wallpaper, which was cracked and peeling in spots. Some of the places were discreetly patched with scotch tape, but Jacob thought that looked pathetic now. He soon fixed the problem, restoring the paper to like-new condition. He bleached the fly-specked ceiling to bright white, and polished the hardwood floor. He made up the bed and fixed the tatters in Papaw's picture. Soon, the brass doorknob glittered like gold, every piece of clothing in the closet became brand new, and the fishbowl became sparkling clear. Even the goldfish looked bigger and brighter. Within minutes, Jacob had changed the room utterly, and he could hardly contain his pleasure.

He knew it couldn't stay like that, of course, and with a disappointed sigh he changed everything back the way it had been before. Almost. He didn't undo the floor polish or the new curtains, and he didn't dirty the fishbowl or dull the goldfish. He also left Papaw's picture alone. He thought those things were small enough that they wouldn't be noticed, and if somebody did notice then he could explain them fairly easily. If he was slow and careful enough, he thought he might even fix the whole house little by little when Mama wasn't paying attention. He had high hopes.

But in the meantime, he slipped the amulet back inside his shirt and got up to go look for Joey. Jacob had been home nearly thirty minutes and he ought to have turned up by now.

He almost skipped the seventh step on his way down before remembering that he didn't have to anymore, then he deliberately set his whole weight on it just to listen to the silence. He fixed two of the worst cracks in the wallpaper and removed a scratch on the bannister without missing a beat, and then slipped through the kitchen as quiet as a whisper to stand hesitating at the entrance to the living room. Mama was still watching her soap, and Jacob waited carefully for a commercial break before clearing his throat.

Mama didn't look back at him.

"What?" she asked irritably.

"Um, I just wondered if you knew where Joey is, Mama," he asked in the humblest and most respectful voice he possessed. Mama hated disrespect above all other crimes.

"I don't know where he is. Go find him yourself if you want him," she said, in a tone that meant the subject was closed. Jacob mumbled something that might have sounded like a thank-you, and then quickly retreated.

He searched rapidly through the house, checking all the places big enough for Joey to be hiding in. He went back upstairs, looking in the hall closet and even venturing into Mama's room. No Joey anywhere. Jacob was beginning to get a little scared, and finally thought of the attic. Joey was afraid to go up there by himself, but he would have known it was the only place he couldn't be found.

Jacob quickly climbed up the narrow steps and poked his head through the door. It was almost too dark to see anything, so he grabbed a rafter in one hand and felt his way forward. There was a little light coming in from the door behind him, and a little more from the louvered windows at each end, so when his eyes adjusted he could make things out a little better. The attic was full of junk which nobody had bothered to clean out in years.

Jacob explored the boxes and piles carefully, and he finally found Joey curled up in a ball in one corner, almost hidden behind stacks and stacks of old yellow newspapers. Jacob could barely see him except when he moved, and he seemed to be making no effort to come out. He realized Joey probably couldn't tell who he was in the dark.

"It's me, Beebo. Come out and tell me what's wrong," he said. That got results. Jacob staggered and barely kept from falling backwards into a mountain of rusty gas pipes heaped up behind him, almost bowled over by what felt like a human cannonball. Joey wouldn't do anything but cry for a long time, and Jacob gave up trying to ask him anything. It could wait.

Instead, he sat down and held him till he stopped crying before trying to talk to him again. Joey still wasn't having any of that just yet, though, and the tears threatened to start all over again.

Eventually he calmed down to the point that Jacob was able to pick him up and carry him out of the attic, and that was progress at least. It wasn't until they came out into the hall that he saw Joey's left eye was almost swollen shut.

Jacob went cold inside. Black eyes don't come from falling- only fists can do that. And the only thing that would make Joey climb up into the attic by himself was the fear of something worse if he didn't.

Jacob said nothing, and took Joey to their room. When he got there, he shut the door and sat down on the bed. He knew, in a way, that this was just as much his fault as it was Mama's, because he was the one who had wanted to go off and leave Joey alone with her. He knew better. He couldn't pretend he didn't.

"Let me look at your eye, Beebo," he whispered. Joey turned his face up, looking at him with one bright blue eye. He couldn't see out of the other one, which gave him a strange, lopsided look.

Jacob didn't care about being secret anymore. He closed his eyes, and imagined Joey's eye the way it was supposed to be, and kissed it. And when he looked again, there was no trace of the black eye left. Joey looked at him soberly and laid his head on his brother's shoulder, and then it was Jacob's turn to cry.

* * * * * * *

"Where'd you go this mornin', Jacob?" Joey asked him finally, when both of them were a little calmer.

"Aw, nowhere," he replied, not wanting to say anything about the amulet or the money either one.

"Yes you did. I saw you cross the pasture and you was gone forever," Joey contradicted. Jacob sighed. So much for secrecy.

"I had to go up to the Rock for a little while, bubba, that's all," he said. That was all Joey really needed to know.

"You stayed gone too long. Mama was mad cause you left and didn't tell her," Joey told him. Jacob tasted a fresh surge of guilt when he heard that.

"I'm sorry, bubba. I won't do that anymore, okay?" he promised. Jacob figured a little humility never hurt anybody, and Joey smiled.

Before either of them could say anything else, they were startled by the sound of the front door slamming, and then the sound of Mama's old green Monte Carlo spinning out of the mudhole it had made in the driveway. Jacob quickly looked out the window to see which way she went.

He saw the car turn north on the highway. There was nothing that direction except a twenty mile drive to the nearest liquor store at the county line, or a little farther to the nearest bar. That meant she wouldn't be back at least for a couple of hours, maybe not even for the rest of the night. Jacob couldn't help feeling a little better now that she was gone.

"Come on, Beebo, let's go clean up the kitchen and make something to eat," he said, with a bit more satisfaction in his voice than he really meant to show. He picked Joey up again and carried him piggyback downstairs to the kitchen. As soon as they got there Jacob sent him into the living room to watch cartoons. He'd learned from experience that Joey usually got in the way more than he helped.

That done, Jacob grabbed a wet dishrag and mopped up the meatball, which had somehow gotten crushed and was now smeared greasily across the floor in a log maroon trail. The empty vodka bottle by the refrigerator was quickly thrown in the trash, and he was in the middle of sweeping up the beer and cigarette butts when he realized there was no reason why he should have to work so hard.

He looked through the door into the living room, where Joey was absorbed in *Tom and Jerry*. He hadn't seemed to think much about what Jacob had done to his eye, but cleaning the kitchen was different.   He might remember that, if he saw anything.   Jacob stealthily reached in his pocket and touched the amulet, then closed his eyes and imagined the kitchen to be spotlessly clean. When he opened them a minute later, you would never have guessed it had ever been messy. Not a speck or a stain was on anything, almost like someone had scrubbed the whole room with a toothbrush.

Jacob laughed to himself again, and started fixing their lunch.

*   *   *   *   *   *   *

There were limits to his power, of course, and over the next few days he gradually discovered what they were. He couldn't affect anything more than about a thousand feet away, and he couldn't create something out of nothing. He couldn't bring things back to life if they were dead, and he couldn't affect anybody's thoughts or feelings.   But he could move things, and he could change one thing into another (if he had the same amount of mass), and he could usually heal wounds on living things and make them grow. He was sure there was still a lot he didn't know.

He often wished the amulet had come with an instruction manual.

If anyone had visited the south side of Jack Mountain about that time, they would have thought something very strange was going on. Jacob remembered what he'd done to the little meadow that first day, and in his enthusiasm he decided to beautify the whole area. He worked unceasingly on the land all round Black Rock, and it gradually became a radically different place than it had ever been before. The first thing he did was to kill all the bugs and snakes and creepy-crawlies. He destroyed every thorn and every thistle, every weed and every wasp. Nothing dangerous or ugly was allowed to invade his little kingdom. It was reserved exclusively for all things bright and beautiful, and he set an invisible barrier to keep any new pests from getting in.

About forty acres was the limit of his power to maintain all this, but within that circle the land was becoming like a page from a fairy tale in which every day is high spring and there is no stain to be found on a single leaf or stone. It was almost perfect now, with only a few little touch-ups remaining.

He was planting white oaks today, setting acorns with one hand and then making them grow into tall trees in less than a minute. He kept one eye on his work and the other on Joey, who was playing in the dirt not far away. Jacob had gradually lost his fear of Mama taking the amulet away from him (*Just let her try*, he said to himself), and as he got bolder he didn't care so much about letting Joey see him do things. So far he seemed to accept it without question, like it was the most natural and ordinary thing in the world, and he hadn't asked how any of it was possible. Jacob was still careful to wear the amulet under his shirt and never mention it, but he was beginning to feel secure in his invincible power. He never took it off anymore, not even when he slept.

He looked down the trail at Joey playing in the dirt, and with a half-smile lifted him off the ground and dusted him off. Joey had loved that at first, but he was getting tired of it.

"Put me down!" he cried, struggling uselessly against the breeze. The sun was beginning to slant low across the ravine, and it was almost time to call it a day.

"I think I might just carry you home that way, Beebo," Jacob replied, teasing him. He wasn't serious, but from Joey's howl you would have thought he was pulling hair. Jacob floated him closer and set him down on his feet.

"I didn't mean it, silly boy," he said, and they walked home with no more ado.

The house looked totally different than it had just a few days ago. Jacob had fixed things the way he liked them, and the whole place looked gleaming and new. Mama couldn't help but notice, but she walked around the house in a daze, not seeming to comprehend what was going on all around her. She knew Jacob was doing it all, but she couldn't figure out how. He never let anyone catch even a glimpse of the amulet, and he never changed anything unless she was gone. If he hadn't known better, he could have sworn he saw fear in her eyes when she looked at him. But whatever she thought, she didn't say anything. Not yet.

There was another reason why she didn't suspect the amulet, though. Jacob had found a safer way to get things done than just wishing them so. He made gold.

It didn't matter what from. He generally picked up a handful of gravel and turned the pieces into nuggets. They always turned out smaller than the pebbles he started with, but that was okay.

He'd tried making diamonds but somehow that never seemed to work right, maybe because he didn't know enough about what he was doing. He could make one, to be sure, but they always seemed to be badly flawed and worthless. He'd taken some of the ones he made to a jewelry shop to ask, and that was what they'd told him. So Jacob gave up on diamonds and stuck to gold. He never had any problems with that.

Selling it for cash had been a real problem at first. Jacob had collected a sack of nuggets that must have weighed twenty pounds, and people tended to get mighty curious about where a fifteen year old kid came up with that much gold.

He'd finally sold his bag of nuggets at a pawn shop. He made a deal with the owner that as long as he asked no questions and paid in cash, Jacob would sell him the gold for half price. The man was no fool, and probably thought he was robbing a kid blind, but Jacob didn't care. He could have built a whole palace of gold if he'd wanted to (well, eventually), so the cut rate didn't annoy him at all.

He stored his cash in one of the old trunks in the attic, where Mama couldn't find it. Some of it he'd spent on things for the house and stuff for him and Joey, but he still had close to eighty thousand dollars stuffed away up there, if he counted right. It was a good feeling, knowing that.

He used his newfound wealth to do all kinds of things he'd never had a chance to do before. He bought anything he wanted, without even looking at the price. He went places and hung out with people who would barely have spoken to him a week ago. Of course he knew most of them liked him because he was generous with his money, but for the time being he honestly didn't care. He was enjoying himself too much.

On Friday night there was a football game at the high school, and Jacob decided to go. Mama was working the night shift, and Jacob had hired a babysitter for Joey, even though he was supposed to be watching him himself. . . something totally unheard of before. Mama probably wouldn't have liked it if she'd known, but Jacob no longer paid any attention to what she thought.

He sat in the front of the stands and cheered as loud as anyone, eating hot dogs and popcorn to his heart's content. He was sorely tempted a few times to make the ball fly just a little farther and help the team score a touchdown, but he didn't meddle.

For the most part. When he saw a chance to make Bobby Lee Jameson fall flat on his face in the mud, Jacob simply couldn't resist. Bobby Lee was the most arrogant, stuck-up bully in the whole school, and Jacob enjoyed getting a chance to make everyone laugh at him for a change. In fact he probably enjoyed it more than he should have, because afterward he felt sorry for doing it.

The game was over at ten, and Jacob decided to walk home for a change. He could have gotten a ride if he wanted one, but he felt like being alone for a while. He paused next to Bobby Lee's old truck in the parking lot and gave him four new mud grip tires and some chrome wheels, to make up for embarrassing him. He'd never know where they came from, but he probably wouldn't question it much either. Jacob felt like things were square between them at that point, and he walked away quickly before anybody noticed him standing there.

The night breezes were cool against his skin, carrying with them the faint scent of late-blooming jasmine from somebody's yard. He felt at peace with himself and and the world, and in the mood to do a good deed if anything happened to present itself. Giving Bobby Lee the tires and wheels had made him wonder what else he might do for other people.

He came to Annie Summerford's house, and on impulse he left a hundred dollar bill in her mailbox. Miss Annie had once been the town librarian, but Jacob knew she was old and poor now. He tried not to carry around a whole lot of cash, but if he lost it he wasn't too worried. He could always get more.

He passed the store and the Baptist church without seeing anything worth doing, and then the graveyard. He removed a smudge of gray lichen from a tombstone, but that wasn't very satisfying. He wanted to do something more dramatic than that.

A few stray leaves were beginning to fall, more from the heat than the season. The colors wouldn't really change much till a little before Halloween, and that was still almost two months away. Winter was a tired beast in these parts.

He crossed the river bridge, and saw his Aunt Carolyn's place was dark and silent beside the river. A few really determined weeds were growing up through her cattle guard, and Jacob quickly killed them for her.

A gibbous moon was shining through the trees behind him, flooding the highway with pools of silver. Jacob waded through them, following his footsteps home. On another day he might have been frustrated by the lack of opportunities to do anything for people. You would think there were more needy folks in the world than just one old woman. But tonight he was feeling good, and it would have taken a lot to darken his mood. Maybe another day, he thought to himself.

He opened the back door and went into the house. The babysitter was on the couch watching a movie, and he paid her and sent her home. Then he locked the door and went up to bed without a sound, not bothering to turn on any lights. There was enough moonlight to see by.

He changed into a more comfortable t-shirt and some shorts, then laid down on the bed beside the already sleeping Joey, listening to the old house creak and settle for the night.

Jacob was happier than he could ever remember being in his whole life, and he foresaw no end to the good times and the good work he could do with the amulet in his hand. He'd barely scratched the surface. He had power and wealth beyond his wildest dreams, and what could he not do now? The amulet had been the greatest thing that ever happened to him.

Jacob smiled, and then slowly drifted off to sleep.

*　*　*　*　*　*　*

In the morning the goldfish was dead.

The bowl had turned gray with pollution, so dense and thick that nothing could be seen through the murk.

Jacob got up and quickly threw it away, promising himself to get a new one in a few days.

He wasn't going to try to pretend it was the same one, but when something died it was usually better to replace it quickly.

He didn't think much about the dead fish at first, but he was soon to get a nasty surprise that gave him plenty of reason to think about it.

It was a glorious Saturday morning in the meantime, though, with just a little scent of fall hanging crisply in the air. It was exactly seven days since he'd first found the amulet, but it seemed to Jacob like that was ages and centuries ago, so far in the past that it was hard to remember. He was happy and felt like going out and doing something.

He changed clothes and woke up his brother.

"Come on, Beebo, get up! Time to go!" he said cheerfully. Joey groaned, and Jacob tried tickling him. That usually worked, but not today. Joey just rolled out of reach and pulled the covers back over his head.

"What's wrong with you, sleepyhead?" Jacob laughed.

"Don't feel good," Joey finally said.

"Well what's wrong? Does your stomach hurt, are you bleeding. . . what is it?" Jacob asked.

"No, just don't feel good," Joey answered. Jacob touched his forehead, but it didn't feel especially warm. Nothing was wrong, as far as he could tell.   Jacob really wanted to go finish growing his trees today, but he knew he couldn't take Joey up there if he was sick, and Mama was working today.

He went downstairs and called Aunt Carolyn to see if she could watch him for a while. She was usually home on Saturdays.

"Sure, I'll be there in a minute," she agreed.

She was, and by the time she got there Jacob had to admit that Joey did look sickly. He was pale and had dark circles under his eyes.

Carolyn took him home with her, and Jacob promised to come fetch him later that afternoon.

He felt a little bit guilty about going off elsewhere when Joey wasn't feeling good, but he told himself Carolyn would take good care of him and it wouldn't be for very long. He sighed and headed up to Black Rock.

Almost as soon as he crossed the invisible barrier between his protected land and the everyday world, he noticed that something wasn't right. Many of the leaves on the trees were yellowed and withered, and some even looked dead. In places he noticed a jelly-like brown fungus growing on the branches, which had certainly not been there before.

Jacob was curious, but not really too worried yet. He used the amulet to kill the fungus and make the plants grow healthy new leaves, but there was nothing he could do about the dead ones. He turned those to dust instead. There were only a few of those, so the gaps were not very noticeable. He worked as he walked along, patiently fixing whatever was messed up.

It was strangely silent in the woods that day, a fact which he didn't notice for quite some time. But presently, as he worked his way up the path, he found a dead cardinal on the ground. It was brilliant red, even more so than normal. Jacob had given it a little extra color at some point, just to make it look nicer. It was hard to say what had killed it. It didn't seem hurt, other than the fact that it was dead. Jacob turned it to dust as he had the withered trees, and it was then that he noticed there were no birdsongs.

All that day, Jacob saw almost nothing living except the trees. He came across several dead or dying birds, and once a dead fox. Jacob had changed all the animals in his little patch of woods in some way or other. . . brightened their colors, made them bigger, given them blue eyes or softer fur or something like that. All of them had been fine yesterday, but now everything seemed to be dying. The trees were withering rapidly, too. Even during the little time he'd spent in the area, the leaves had yellowed and dropped off a large number of them. Even the grass was dying, and Jacob was finally starting to get worried.

He fought hard against the spreading destruction that had dropped like a stone into his peaceful kingdom, until he was exhausted from the battle. He couldn't keep up. Barely did he grow a new tree before it began to die too, and within an hour it was a dead trunk like so many others. He tried healing a few of the birds that were still alive and found that it lasted only a few minutes before the bird was dead. Jacob was at his wit's end, unable to figure out what was happening or how he could stop it. His beloved sanctuary was beginning to look like a wasteland.

By sundown, there was nothing left but dead sticks and bare dust, like a bomb had exploded and destroyed every living thing.

Just as the sun slipped below the horizon, Jacob abruptly gave up all hope of doing any more good up there. He ran down the trail towards home, paying no more attention to the dead and blasted region he had spent so much effort to cultivate.

When he got home, he went directly to the phone. All he cared about right now was getting hold of Aunt Carolyn, because a horrible new fear had gripped his mind. He got her voice mail three times, and that only made it worse.

He left the house, running down the road to his aunt's place as fast as he could go. There was no car in the driveway, but he hoped against hope that maybe somebody was home, that maybe Carolyn had just gone to the store for something. He came to the front door, still breathing hard from his run, and found a note pinned to the mailbox. He snatched it, and slowly read what was written there.

Jacob, if you read this, we're gone to the hospital. Joey is very sick. I already called your mother and she's coming up here. Stay home and we'll try to call you later.

That was all it said, but that was enough. Because he knew what was wrong by now, without a doubt. Every living thing he'd touched with the amulet had sickened and died, and he had used it on Joey to heal his black eye.

Which he wouldn't have had in the first place, if Jacob hadn't been so careless. So whose fault would it really be, if he. . .

Jacob couldn't bring himself to even finish thinking that thought, and he sat down on Carolyn's porch and wept for the second time in a week.

Presently he went home and sat in the gleaming kitchen beside the phone, anxious not to miss any calls. He soon found that doing nothing was unbearable, so he fixed a frozen pizza and ate as much of it as he had the heart for. Then he wandered slowly through the quiet rooms in silence, touching things here and there. The house was like a palace now, almost. Jacob hadn't refused himself anything he wanted, from marble floors to crystal chandeliers, and anything and everything in between. It didn't seem so wonderful now, and he would have gladly traded all of it just to have Joey home safe. What were money and things, compared to that?

Eventually Carolyn did call, and the news wasn't good. Joey was still hanging on, but just barely, and she said he might not make it till morning. Jacob stayed calmer at that news than he thought he would. It might have been because he already expected it, or it might have been because some things are too terrible even for tears. Maybe both.

He got off the phone with his aunt not long after that. He felt dead inside, and couldn't think of anything else to say. He knew he must have seemed heartless, but right then he didn't have the heart to care.

Jacob pulled the amulet out from under his shirt and looked at it with hatred, wishing he'd never found it in the first place. If Joey died then Jacob would never forgive himself. He studied the medallion forlornly, praying that he might find something new to show him a way to save his brother. But the only things he saw were the gleaming silver and the seven bright gems, and the flowing script around the edge.

Jacob seized on the writing. He'd never cared what it said before, because it didn't seem to matter much. But now those unreadable words became the most important thing in the world, because they were the only clue he had. Jacob quickly wrote them down on paper. There were three lines, and the writing was tiny. He had to get out a magnifying glass to make sure he spelled them right.

As soon as he had them, the first thing he did was go to his computer. It was brand new, just bought two days ago with some of the cash from the gold. Jacob had barely had time to even look at it yet, but it had Internet access, and that was all he cared about.

He found a language translation website, where he quickly tried all the languages it offered, with no luck. The language on the amulet wasn't Latin, or Spanish, or French, or German, or Italian, or Portuguese, or Dutch. Jacob knew it wasn't Japanese or Arabic, because it was written with letters that were familiar to him, and those languages wouldn't have been.

He made a list of all the languages that were normally written with Roman letters, no matter how obscure they were, then crossed off the ones he'd already tried. He was left with about ten he'd actually heard of before and maybe twice that many he hadn't. But which one was it? And what if it was some dead language nobody even spoke anymore?

As a last resort, he posted the words on an Internet message board about languages, asking what language they were and what they meant, and in the meantime he kept looking, without success.

Thirty minutes later, a girl halfway around the world answered his question. Jacob opened the message as fast as his fingers could click the mouse, and this is what he read:

> *The language is Magyar, very old. It says "Seven days you have the power. Touch no living thing. If the chain is broken, all is lost," Where you find this, buddy?*

Jacob didn't try to answer that question. The girl wouldn't have believed him anyway. He wished bitterly that he'd known those three things a week ago.

Except, of course, he knew he *could* have known a week ago, if he'd only made the effort to try. But he'd been careless about that too, and because of his carelessness Joey might die.

Jacob thought he knew what to do now though, if he understood the words right. He prayed to God he wasn't wrong. He took the necklace of the amulet in both hands, closed his eyes, and then, with a hard yank, he snapped the chain.

As always, there was no fanfare, nothing to show that the magic had worked. Jacob heard and felt nothing except the breaking of the silver chain. He opened his eyes, and found himself sitting on a stool in the attic, still holding the two tarnished ends of the necklace in his hands. The trunk where he'd found it a week ago was open in front of him, and the cigar box was sitting on the corner.

Jacob blinked stupidly, and had a surge of déjà vu so strong that he honestly wasn't sure what was real and what wasn't anymore. He stood up, and found that he was wearing the same clothes he wore last Saturday, and he was barefooted. He put the amulet in his pocket absentmindedly, and threaded his way through the junk until he reached the door. Then he went downstairs. He hardly dared to hope.

He opened his bedroom door slowly. Everything was just as it had always been before he found the amulet. There was no trace of all the changes he'd made. Jacob crept to the bed, still barely believing it, and pulled the edge of the blanket down.

There was Joey, still asleep with his thumb in his mouth, just the way he'd been when Jacob left him to go up to the attic last week. Rain was beating in heavy sheets against the window glass.

Jacob had to pinch himself to make sure he wasn't dreaming. He still didn't believe it and pinched himself again. Did "all is lost" mean even the time that had passed since he found the amulet? Apparently so.

Jacob finally decided he didn't care two cents about how or why it worked. Joey was back, and he was safe, and that was all that mattered. Joey made a vague sleepy sound and moved closer to him, not really awake. He settled comfortably against Jacob's side and grew quiet again. He was dreaming about something from the way his eyes moved, and Jacob smoothed down a cowlick in his soft golden hair with one hand.

"Love you, Beebo," Jacob whispered, and then he laid down next to his sleeping brother and held him close for a long time.

Jacob never forgot that lost week. No one else remembered a bit of it, and there were times when Jacob himself started to wonder if he hadn't dreamed the whole thing. But when such times came, he only had to look at the amulet and hold it in his hand, and he was sure. It was powerless now, but he fixed the chain and always wore it from then on, to remind him of the things that really matter. And that was the best magic of all.

The Way of Zoë

A Tale of Hope

Methought the billows spoke and told me of it,
The winds did sing it to me,
And the thunder, that deep and dreadful organ
pipe. . .

-William Shakespeare,
The Tempest

The Way of Zoë

Once, in a little mountain hollow, there lived a young girl by the name of Delores. She was not specially beautiful, except in the way that a kind heart is beautiful, and she was not witty, nor charming, nor rich, nor any of the other things that men seek after. She seldom laughed (for she had known much sorrow in the world), but her smile was as warm as the sun on the bright yellow daffodils that grew in the meadow in springtime.

Her father had died long ago and left his family quite poor, with only the little plot of land and the little white house in the dell. Her mother sold sachets of herbs in the town, and this was how they lived.

And so it was that Delores would often walk alone through the fields and the forest in her little bare feet and her old blue print dress, to gather flowers and herbs for her mother. And often as not, her tears would fall freely to water the bouquet she carried.

"What is it that hurts you so much, Delores?" her mother would ask sometimes, for she was a tender and gentle old soul.

"Oh, mama, I wish I could tell. . . but all I know is how sad all the pretty things seem," Delores said. And this was true (for she was a truthful girl), but there was more to the ache in her heart than that.

She *wished* for something. . . but she never could see what it was. A formless and bittersweet longing possessed her, which nothing seemed to satisfy; it was a hope with no object she knew of, but still she couldn't let it go. And when something appeared, like the golden spring flowers, to remind her of this unknown thing, the tears welled up with a life of their own.

She could not have found words to explain any of this without feeling very foolish and (even worse) distressing her mother with a burden that no one could help. So Delores kept her thoughts to herself, and let her tears fall only in solitude. And if now and then people noticed her sadness and silence, they had the good grace to say nothing about it.

Years passed in this way, and then one day while she walked in the woods on a cool early morning in March, with a little clutch of daffodils clasped in her hand and a light breeze tickling the nape of her neck, she came upon a dove lying still in the path. She saw feathers scattered round, and his wing bent back at an awkward angle, broken. Perhaps a cat had been after him, she thought. She felt an instant pity for the poor thing, and if her cheeks had not already been wet they soon would have been.

Delores carefully picked him up, feeling his heart beat so rapidly she feared it would burst. He trembled in her hand, but her tears washed the dirt from his wing, and in a moment he stretched it forth, unbroken after all, and flew to a nearby bush. Delores was so startled by this that she forgot to cry.

"What happened?" she wondered out loud, staring at the bird curiously.

"With your tears you have healed me," the dove said to her in a piping little voice that reminded her of whistles. Delores had never been spoken to by an animal before and didn't know quite what to think, but she smiled timidly.

"Come follow me!" the dove urged her, and turned to fly away. Delores took a small step after him, then another, and after that it was easy to go on.

She had lived in the hollow all her life, but the dove soon led her into places she did not recognize at all. After a long time they came to an old stone wall, weathered and crumbling in places. There didn't seem to be any way to go on, so Delores stopped in front of it.

"Come on, come on!" the dove called to her from a perch atop the wall, bobbing his head encouragingly. Delores looked up at him, frowning.

"There's no gate, and the wall is too high for me to climb," she told him, a little crossly.

"You have to find a way to go on, child, and when you do you will be glad," the bird promised her. Delores considered it, and with a sigh began piling loose rocks against the wall. Soon they were high enough to let her scramble up on top, and what she saw on the other side astonished her.

A wild and weedy garden stretched as far as she could see, full of flowers and trees and little rock paths that seemed to lead nowhere, with stray blades of grass pushing up between the stones. One of the trees grew quite close to the wall, and after a moment Delores gave in to curiosity, climbing down the trunk to the ground.

Now she could see that of all the flowers in the garden, no two were alike, and every tree was a different kind. And there were butterflies, too- a thousand colors and shapes, that danced in the sunlight all around her. She held out her hand and a bright blue one settled there, tickling her finger. Delores smiled with delight, enchanted.

She took another step on the little rock path, more confident now, and looked for the dove. He was nowhere to be seen, but Delores soon spied something much more interesting.

Not far away grew a Tree so magnificent that it immediately made everything else in the garden seem dull and ordinary in comparison. Its bark was silver-gray, and upon it grew the reddest, most perfect apples you ever imagined. Delores didn't stop to think how strange it was to see apples ripe in March. The beautiful Tree attracted her powerfully, and she set out to reach it at once.

It was not as close as it had looked, but as she walked Delores began to observe that everything in the garden was arranged around that one Tree. What had looked like wild ruin from the outside began more and more to reveal a kind of order she had not suspected was there. And there was something else, too.

It was so subtle that she did not notice it at first, but the closer she came to the Tree the stronger it became, and when she touched the smooth silver bole even her sad young heart could feel it. There was joy in the garden, so full and so deep that it was simply impossible to have a sad or a fearful thought while you were there. There was no room for those things any more; the joy had washed them all away. She who had so often wept at the bitter longing in her soul now felt her heartache fulfilled, and all her sorrow dissolved away like salt in cool water.

Delores might willingly have basked in the sweet and loving shelter of the Tree forever, but after a little while she remembered her mother, sitting at home in her rocker, waiting patiently for Delores' return. It was long past time to be home.

The garden was very, very quiet, except for the faint rustling of the wind in the leaves and the grass, and when her hand left the trunk of the Tree the thought of leaving seemed suddenly unbearable. Tears filled her eyes when she took the first step, though the honey taste of joy still wrapped her about. The idea that she would never touch that happiness again filled her with desolation sharp as splinters, for she knew she would never find the way without the dove.

Before she had gone another step he was beside her.

"Don't cry, beloved child. No good thing is ever lost. I would never have brought you here otherwise. Someday I'll come to you, and lead you here again. But go now, take an apple from the Tree, and as often as you hold it in your hands, then sadness will never touch your heart any more," he whispered.

Delores thought of that, and smiled through her tears. She reached out for one of the bright apples, and plucked it from the Tree as the dove had told her.

At once the garden vanished from around her, and she found herself standing alone, high up on the mountain, with the hollow spread out like a green pool of velvet at her feet. The wind was blowing, and the faint scent of pine needles wafted up from below. She could almost believe she had imagined the dove and the garden, but when she looked down she saw that she still clasped the red, red apple in her hand.

Delores smiled, softly, and set off down the mountain with a spring in her step and fresh color in her cheeks. And she began to sing as she went, in her high clear voice, the merriest tunes the old hollow ever heard. She was beautiful then, with all the sweet beauty of goodness and joy.

Many years passed for Delores in happiness, and sorrow could not touch her, nor anyone she loved. The apple stayed fresh, and red as the cardinal's breast, and whenever she touched it the joy of the garden surrounded her again.

And when she had grown to be a very old lady, and lived all alone in the little white house, with fingers she barely could clasp in prayer, there came one night in March a slight sound at her door. She opened it slowly, and there in the warm spring night was the dove.

"I've waited for you, always," Delores whispered, and picked him up tenderly in her frail old hands.

"Will you come with me, child, to the garden again?" he said to her softly. Delores smiled quickly and said "Yes. . . oh, yes."

And the dove led her off through the sweet woods and meadows, where the pines and the daffodils grew, and somewhere a path began that led far away.

And behind them, unnoticed in the little white house, the red, red apple faded slowly to nothing.

The Ballad

of Sarah de Bretagne

A Tale of Love

Many waters cannot quench love, neither can the floods drown it.

– Song of Solomon 8:7

Canto I

The rains fell down,

And the black floods came,

And there in the dark stood Sarah Cymru.

Lightning snarled on Snowdon's ragged breast,

The rain driving hard as flint arrows

Against the mountains and the sea.

A lone ship stood at anchor,

In the ashen bay of Aberffraw,

Starkly illumined by the town in flames.

There stood Meriadoc, Lord of Gwynedd;

She watched his grieved glances up the green rocky fells,

In search of the daughter who tarried too long.

But she stood with numbed soul and came not.

Pale face haggard with freshwater tears,

She saw his hand fall, though she heard not his cry;

The little ship struggled in sea of high swells,

Like broken blue pottery gnashing its teeth.

And then it was gone, to the south far away,

While Aberffraw died in the harsh driving rain.

Sarah shivered with dread, but did steel her strong arm;

The Saxons were coming; there was naught else to do.

With narrowed blue eyes did she set her bare feet,

On the twisting tortured downward path,

Turning her back on ancient Gwynedd.

There was none left but her and the hated invaders:

Time only would tell of the victor this night,

She swore with a grimness beyond her scant years.

Gripping the hilt of her Toledo-sharp dirk,

For hours she crept through the Cambrian dark,

Shivering and soaked in her plaid robes of state,

Which she knew all too well did mark her as prey.

She drew near the town, heard shrieking of dogs,

And ribald carousing through thick castle walls.

She smiled a wintry smile, baring even white teeth,

And slid through the garden over trampled wet beds,

To a secret back way only royals knew.

She slipped like cold breath into Roderick Caer;

By devious means did she reach the main gate,

Shut fast for the night against aught which might come,

Whether animal, spirit, or Celtic avenger.

With a flick barely heard, she jammed the old lock…

No one was leaving; least of all her.

None saw her, none stopped her, so careful she crawled,

While the men partied on unbeknowing in bliss.

A barrel of mead and a torch in the rushes –

Caer Roderick Mawr was aflame!

They rushed for the gate – The fools! She exulted;

And they screamed in stark terror at facing sweet Death.

She stepped on the dais and drew herself up;

"It was I who destroyed you killers and thieves!"

She cried like a fiend as she brandished her blade.

They shrank from before her, so occult she seemed,

A demon of Hades come claiming their souls.

With a cold heart she watched as they fell down and died,

And the flames licked up at the hem of her gown.

The brocade swift blackened, caught fire and cracked;

She smiled with fierce triumph and gripped her cold steel.

With a swift practiced motion it plunged toward her breast,

And she welcomed the pang ere it came.

But a pale white hand seized the blade in her grasp,

And was cut to the bone; she heard a wild curse;

Blood splattered to sizzle on the smoking stone floor,

While the dagger skittered down in the flames.

In a rage she lunged after it, straining to die,

But two arms held her back till she finally broke,

Then hauled her in haste out the royal way.

Through the ruin of tulips and roses and trees,

Where she'd played as a girl within sight of the sea,

Away from Caer Roderick down the muddy black beach.

Sea creatures slithered and writhed on the sands,

Dying in slime on the alien shore,

Where the night storm had cast them, alone and afar;

There was their tomb, and she envied such peace.

She knew not the way; she no longer cared;

Her brain was a mass of wet clay in her head;

She spoke not a word, but neither did he;

Whether Saxon or Brython she knew not, nor cared.

Yet his hand on her arm was gentle and light,

Never forcing nor hurting nor pulling away,

But utterly firm and unyielding as marble.

The flames of Caer Roderick faded away,

And the lightning abated with muttering scowls;

A sliver of moon pushed brave through the clouds,

Till her pale red hair was all gilded in silver,

And she looked every year of the hundred she felt.

They came to a cave on the black sea strand,

Just a jumble of rocks all crusted with white,

And there the man built up a bower of stone,

For to hold the Celt maiden he so long had loved;

She lay without protest and closed her blue eyes,

Hands folded regally cross on her breast,

A pale colored orchid by the dark gray sea,

Or so did she seem to the Prince at her feet.

And then he lay down by her side in the dark,

Debated, then tenderly kissed her wet hair;

No more did he venture, nor yet did he wish,

And together they slept in the stones by the sea.

Canto II

The golden sun in the morn uprist,

To flood the dark beach with a warm red wave,

Where the Prince of Anjou and the Celt maiden lay,

Alone with the sea and the dead of the storm.

The sky feathered blue like cormorants' wings,

And salty white foam raced the waves on the shore.

He looked up and smiled at the watercolor sky,

And thanked the dear Lord for his love and his life,

So near come to perishing yesterday night.

He turned to the maiden that lay at his side,

Tenderly open while yet she still slept,

And whispered *"Je t'adore, ma chère et ma vie."* [1]

Perhaps through the cold of her broken-glass heart,

She heard the soft words, for she opened her eyes,

To behold Prince Guillaume looking down from so near,

And he longed to say more, but naught else could be said.

"Who art thou?" she asked him, "to pry in my plans?

Speak swiftly, young man, thou hast much to explain."

The prince's heart sighed at the ice in her tone,

But he gathered his thoughts to reply as he must.

"My name is Guillaume of Anjou in France,

But the days of my youth have I passed in Gwynedd,

In the house of thy father Meriadoc the King.

I saw thee each day at Caer Roderick Mawr,

In the garden of blossoms where Beauty doth dwell,

And I watched thee, and listened, heard tell of so much;

Saw thee dancing in springtime on daisies new-sprung,

Where the sweet blue-grey mist lit on rolling green hills,

And thou smiled in the sunshine that clothed thee in light;

Such a sweetness I saw that I wished in my heart,

And did call thee *ma chère* [2] in my dearest of dreams,

Though I thought not to ever speak words such as these. . .

But then came the Saxons with terrible War;

Thy father Meriadoc quit these high coasts,

With all of the people his tongue could persuade;

Even I, but not thee, I could tell in my bones.

I knew all thy moods and did feel them the same,

So remained in Caer Roderick hid in the hall,

Whilst the last ship weighed anchor in Aberffraw bay,

For I knew thou wouldst come, and what thou wouldst do.

I waited and watched as the Saxons caroused,

And grew drunk on the fat of thy father's rich land;

When thou camest in secret I followed each step,

Till the moment should come when I knew I must act;

Here is my hand. . . thou knowest the rest."

And with difficult silence he heard her reply.

"Thou art bold and unwise to say such to me.

Did I ask for thy help, much less for thy love?

Thou knowest me not, but art kind nonetheless;

Dear Boy, leave me be; thou wist not what thou wishest."

And the stone in her voice left naught to discuss.

A spray of salt wind brought a tear to his eye,

"S'il te plaît, ma plus chère," [3] he promised, but then,

She reached out a pitying hand to his breast.

Her thin white fingers lay warm on his heart;

Close-bitten nails catching rough on his shirt.

"Thou'rt good to me, truly; I know it, dear friend,

Though I meet thee at times and in ways I wish not. . .

Go back to Anjou of the emerald south,

And find there an other more suited to thee."

These kind words spake she with a dull timbred voice,

Wishing for something. . . anything else.

"And where wilt thou go, fair maiden beloved?

Caer Roderick Mawr and Gwynedd are now lost,

And naught may restore them or give life again,

To memories sweeter than present days know.

Thou art lovely and good; how it stabs me to think

Thou wouldst cast away life for the sake of revenge.

Oh, say thou wilt not!" he beseeched with a cry.

She drew her breath sadly and cast down her gaze.

"Ah, 'twas not for revenge that I did what I did.

'Twas merely for glory, and justice, and pride.

Thou hast made these impossible now the deed's done;

Thou hast nothing to fear for my death anymore.

I go to Bretagne where Meriadoc rules,

No more to look back on these mountains I love.

There will I dance, as I did in the Caer,

Princess and bauble, for such I will be,

Till Meriadoc finds better uses for me.

Marriage, perchance, to some warty old Lord,

At the court of Gascon, or even Anjou. . .

Say where is the romance and honor in that?

But such is the life thou returns't me," she sighed,

Shaking her head so her rippled hair danced,

As she sat up to gaze at the whispering sea.

Sun licked the waves with goldenrod fleece,

And did taste of the deep with ephemeral lips.

Sarah rose up and soon smoothed her fair plaids,

Still lovely, though battered and burned at the hems.

Then barefoot she set out to find a sweet pool,

For to drink and refresh herself thence for the walk,

To Llanfaelog-town where the fisher-folk dwelt.

Mayhap one remained who could bear her away.

Guillaume followed after in silence profound.

Canto III

They wended their path to Llanfaelog-town,
Whence a grizzled old fishwife did ferry them south,
To Aberyst-wyth whence the trade ships would ply,
To Santander and Erin, the Baltic, and France.
From thence would they go on their disparate ways,
And meet nevermore in the world till the end.
But the country was fair while they waited to leave,
In the last blush of summer they'd feel in Gwynedd.
There were naught but each other they knew in the town,
And solitude came all too quickly, they felt,
So they walked the long valley the Aeron had cut,
In the bones of the mountains of Cambria's coast,

And they spoke of the past and exchanged mighty tales,

Over cheese and wine lunches on August-green grass,

In the depths of the forest where no one could hear.

Guillaume did not speak of his love any more,

For fear of distressing her sore troubled brow,

But it shone through in other ways subtle and dear,

For true it still was, and he wished her all joy.

Then the hour came at last, on Michaelmas Day,

That the two of them met for the very last time.

The first taste of Autumn hung crisp in the air,

While they told funny stories to cheer their farewells.

But as they sat on a log by the Aeron's stone banks,

Sarah finally stopped laughing, and turned to Guillaume

With a serious mein, and unburdened her heart.

"How art thou so happy, and kind and carefree,

When we both see such evil that crusheth the soul?

Understand thee I cannot, unless thou knowest nothing,

But that too is impossible; thou art a riddle.

Pray tell me thy secret. . . I fain would hear now."

Her open face waiting, he hardly could think.

"I know not exactly what words I should say,.

But I'll sing thee a ballad, a tale of Anjou,

Which my father did tell me the day I left home.

Perhaps it will help thee; if not, then I'll show thee,"

He promised with gentleness, care in his tone.

He drew in his breath, sat up straight and looked down,
In her bright blue eyes and began then to sing.

"Ah, je te souhaite de la grande joie, mon fils!
Écoutez, donc, car je chante du sagesse:
L'amour et la vie et tes songes et le vrai,
Ceux seulement sont nobles d'aimer dans l'enfin:
Quand la vie est facile, laissez les bons temps rouler!
Souvenez d'amour vrai ne peut mourir jamais." [4]

He finished the last with a half-hidden grin.
"Oh, indeed?" Sarah scoffed with a roll of her eyes,
"Well, I'll tell *thee* the story that life has taught me,
And I believe it more true than thy pithy refrain.
People care only for power and wealth;
Happiness comes as an afterthought. . . maybe.
A good man I liken to fresh wine in June,
All sweet and delicious; so lovely at first!
But when kept overlong merely souring to vinegar.
Love is a waste, and fools only dream,
And what is the Truth? Do you still think you know?
Life is not easy and never will be;
Wisdom and happiness poison each other;
Thou canst not have one and retain still the former.
I know, for I've tried, and in time so wilt thou."

She asserted these doctrines with angry sad eyes,

Tossing pebbles to *crack!* on the stones down below.

At a loss what to say, he embraced her thin shoulders;

She stiffened, then yielded and patted his arm.

"Ah, thy friendship doth cheer me, though foolish it be.

A good man thou art; I prithee change not."

She spake the words softly; he nodded and said,

"Once did I believe these same words thou dost say,

For I saw such vile cruelty, hatred, and greed. . .

Lecherous fools and rich thieves in Le Havre,

While children stood starving not ten yards away;

Such dirt and blood and filth unspeakable!

It angered me sore, and I called the world cursed,

And the hot breath of hell near to broke my sad heart.

I could not do aught to relieve all the pain,

For the world changeth not, and loveth no man.

But dear one, I tell thee, there's more than I knew!

All thou hast said, it is true, I agree,

But such wisdom is half-truth, and kills all joy.

Yet, 'tis all thou canst see, alone with no hope.

My song helped not, but I promised I'd show thee

The answer thou seekest. . . other ways will I try.

So follow and listen, observe every thing;

Take note of the tiny, the subtle, the plain,

For this is the heart and the blood of all joy.

Come now, *ma chère*, let us dither no more;

For I've much I must show thee, and ah what short time!"

They got up and walked through the green Aeron vale,

Side by side in the aisles of leafy grey beeches;

The river splashed laughingly cool at their right,

Kissing the air with glittering spray,

Like diamond dust scattered through lead crystal glass,

And the warm west wind blew its breath at their backs.

Canto IV

They chanced upon a butterfly, caught in a pool of rain;

Guillaume shook his head and reached down with his fingers

To lift it up, free, to the zephyr's embrace.

It flew away shining in dappled gold light.

"Thy freedom I grant thee, for such is the gift,

Of all living creatures the Lord ever made!"

He called with a smile, then turned to the girl.

"When thou findest the needy, though tiny they be,

Neglect not to help them, though aught tell thee no.

Reach out and heal every hurt in thy sight,

From the death of an insect to tears of a stranger.

This is worth much; deceptively so."

He assured her obliquely, and quickened his stride.

They came to a cliff overlooking the vale,

And there Guillaume sat on the cool earthen floor.

Wild roses bloomed in the sheltered wet nooks,

Confused by the warmth of the south-facing stone,

Smiling and nodding at Sarah, serene.

The prince reached a hand for the reddest in sight,

With petals of velvet and scent of high spring.

Then he laughed for no reason and offered it her;

She smiled, just a little, and sat down as well.

The flower she wove in the hair by her ear,

 A splash of wet crimson to rival the dawn.

"These flowers bloom only in May in Gwynedd,

And yet, here they are, without fear for the day!

We could not have known they were coming, but still,

They made thee to smile. . . take thought for this matter.

The greatest of joys are not planned, *chère amie,*

But surprise with delight unexpected and sweet."

And they stole on still farther and reached a great tree,

A handsome old oak, and there Guillaume stopped

And took Sarah's hand in his own without smiling.

She allowed this, uncertain, and waited for more.

"And there also is this, the very last thing,

By far the most crucial and hardest to take.

All that I do, which thou call'st kind and good,

'Twill soon be forgotten; 'tis thankless and hard,

And surprises be hateful as often as not.

This thou wilt find, if thou believest my words.

But this mattereth not, for 'tis done for Another.

These are the gifts which I offer in love,

To Him who breathed life in this body of clay.

He hath blessed me with joy, and filled me with love,

And the more I pour out, the more do I have!

Remember thy faith, my fairest beloved;

Naught else avails long, if thou lack'st this one thing."

And with that he fell silent and cast down his eyes.

Sarah hardly could find any words to reply,

Till the moment he kissed the soft hand in his grasp.

She sighed with old pain and drew it away.

"Guillaume. . . do not do this; I pray thee to stop.

I never can give thee the love that thou wishest,

I have seen far too much, and remember old wounds.

'Twould pain me to hurt thee. . . pray cease and forgive.

If thou lovest me truly, ask not any more."

And she fled down the path by the cold laughing stream,

Heedless of aught but the sound of her feet.

Willow-wands flogged her and left tiny welts,

To bleed tears of blood down her smooth and dry cheeks.

She ran till the pain in her powdered left side,

Made her halt by the Aeron to quiet her breath.

She listened behind for the sound of his steps,

But the valley was silent as soft falling snow.

Her breath at last calmed, and the hurt drained away;

The blood on her face she washed clean in the stream.

Then she gathered her will from its scattered abodes,

And walked more sedately toward Aberyst-wyth.

Within hours her ship would depart over sea,

And mayhap a few worries she'd leave far behind.

Mayhap it were so; she prayed it might be.

Her footfalls were light as the grass in the spring,

And left not a trace of her passage behind;

It was almost as if, to the Cambrian hills,

She had ceased to exist on that night in the Caer;

Her land had forgotten her ere she could leave.

The thought made her sad, but she crushed such a weakness;

She was a Princess; that still meant a bit.

Her father might scold, or he might praise her courage

For all she had done; one could never be sure,

But mattered it really so much, after all?

Whichever he chose, naught would change in the main.

Sarah came to the town on her silent cat's feet,

Took her path to the quay and soon found her good ship,

Bound for Santander by way of grey Brest.

From thence would she follow the vale of Elorn,

To the high rocky fastness her father had built,

In the side of a peak in les Montagnes d'Arreé.

While the sailors cast off and the land dropped away,

She stood on the deck looking back at Gwynedd,

And all it contained, and all she had been.

The breeze blew her hair in a cloud of pale red,

And the bloom she'd forgotten fell down from her ear.

It lay on the deck for a moment in time,

An out-of-place prettiness already near fading.

She held back at first, then took it in hand,

And thoughtfully drew in the scent of past sweetness.

She lingered above till the coast slipped astern,

Then, holding her blossom, at last turned away.

Canto V

He listened a while till the sound of her running,

Faded away in the afternoon quiet,

And all the bright world was left breathless and waiting,

For what should come next, which naught could reveal.

A late singing robin called out from above,

Then hushed as if thinking of Autumn so near.

The sun went on shining, wild roses growing,

Aeron still chattered nonsensical tunes,

While Guillaume could do nothing but inwardly scream,

Or chase her, or weep, and he knew none would help.

He fell to his knees for a prayer forlorn,

The worn mountain stones digging harsh in his legs,

But he paid them no mind with his sorrow so fresh.

The old oak washed him with comforting shade,

Caressing his brow like a cooling wet cloth,

While the wind on the water sang prettily on,

Of things he knew not; cared no more to imagine.

He rose from the ground with a shuddering sigh,

Looked longingly westward, then turned slow away.

A rain cold and gray began to fall from the sky,

Though the day had seemed fair just a little before.

With his fists clenched in balls till his fingernails hurt,

He climbed the long vale toward the ancient grey hills,

Till it closed up about him like wrinkled rock hands,

And he reached a high cliff where the Aeron fell down,

In a thunder of spray from the rounded old crags.

The high-soaring walls formed a chancel of green,

A granite cathedral more lovely than marble,

Fluted with water-shapes, carved organ pipe-stones,

Half-melted faces of monsters and men.

He could go on no farther and halted a bit,

To think what to do, but naught came to mind.

Algae-strewn boulders lolled drunkenly round,

Near sunken in foam as it swirled from the falls,

And to one of these couches Guillaume at last moved.

Leaping nimble and fearless by broken-up rills,

Which raged underfoot like a rabid white bear,

He gained a great boulder and lay on his side,
Looking down at the water reflecting the sky,
And felt the wet stone seeping cold in his bones.
Wind whipped the spray in a fine misty quilt,
That fell on his face like the summertime dew.
He took a deep breath, scenting earth and wet wood,
From the rain and the spray that thin-coated his throat.
The thread of a song flowed clean through his head,
And a sweet tuneless melody spilled from his lips,
Half-remembered from childhood in distant Anjou,
Half sprung from the seed of his own dreamer's mind.
He tinkered a while till the work pleased his ear,
And then sang aloud by the roar of the falls.

Les fleurs sont sauvage, et rouge dans la pluie,
Mais belle, quand le monde est sombre et gris,

Leur beauté je tenis serré à mon coeur,
Ici dans la pluie sans la dame qui j'adore.

Et je chante à moi-même dans ce pays-ci lointain,
Touchant toi, la belle fille avec mon coeur dans sa main,

C'est dur, et mes yeux bleus sont gris comme la pluie,
Qui tombe froid et triste dans ce pays désolé,

Ah oyez, ma chère, mon coeur est cassé!
Mais je t'aimerai vraiment pour jamais et jamais. . . [5]

He faded to tremolo, faded away,

Fell silent and wept on the stone in the stream,

But quietly still, for he hated to cry.

There was no one to hear in the Cambrian wilds,

But that was no reason to lose self-control.

At length he arose to retrace his goat's path,

Through the rocky fall pool to the carven rock bank.

He reached it in safety and followed the trail,

Through the mossy beech wood of the green Aeron vale,

Till he reached the old oak tree, rustling with pity.

He passed without stopping the patch of wild roses;

The torn-away stem of the flower he'd picked,

Looked reproachfully up with a beaded sap eye.

He couldn't look back; it had been such a waste.

He drew near the log where scant hours past,

He'd spoken with Sarah of happiness' ways;

Now he wondered if really he'd been such a fool.

Was she right after all? If so, what despair!

He kicked the log viciously, hurt his big toe,

Cursed and then prayed for forgiveness at once.

Then he limped down the valley to Aberyst-wyth,

Where his own ship awaited, he knew all too well.

Must needs he go to Le Havre, he supposed,

Though he hated that place, with its thieving and filth.

From thence to Anjou it was not very far,

And what then? He wondered, but cared not to ponder.

His father would surely have something in mind;

Boring at best, and most likely distasteful.

Five years in Gwynedd had turned out so, at least.

Ah, that isn't true, he thought with regret;

It was worth every moment I spent with the maiden.

"Whichever way thou goest, may Fortune thence follow!"

He called to her silently, quoting old Virgil.

He thought she'd approve that, if ever she knew.

Fitting it seemed, this farewell *ex post facto.* [6]

He boarded his ship, shook the dirt from his boots,

And never looked back, except in his dreams,

Till the moment he'd meet his fair maiden again.

Canto VI

She landed in Brest on a cool autumn day,

While the ocean lay brooding and stormy beneath;

Reflecting the state of her mind, perchance.

So she liked to imagine, poet she was.

Bretagne seemed no different than home that day,

And she thanked God for that. . . a little, at least.

She knew she could send for a guard any moment,

Arrive in Caer Lache with comfort and pomp,

Be welcomed with love as the prodigal child,

But she wished not to do this; it rankled her freedom.

She was a Princess, and *ought* to be free.

Then she thought of the sight she must make at that moment,

Two months in one garment, all sea-worn and penniless;

Ragged and dirty she stood on the wharf,

Like a kitchen-work drudge in her Lady's old gown.

She laughed at the image with humorous rue;

How silly it was, to care for such things!

She'd had time to reflect on the long ocean trip,

Alone with her thoughts and the words of Guillaume,

And decided (perhaps) life might not be so grim.

Not always, in all; just more often than not.

She thought she could live on the rarities now.

She touched the wild rose that lay deep in her pocket,

Feeling the texture of velvety spring,

And thought, *Yes, perhaps; at least I have this.*

She wished she'd not run quite as soon as she had;

It was almost a reflex she almost regretted.

Not quite, for she still had no faith in such love

As he proffered to give, though he shook her disbelief.

Now he was gone it was safe to regret,

And cherish the moments the flower kept fresh.

She would never forget him, she promised herself,

And would warm the cold nights by the light of her memory.

She wished he could know this, but dared not to tell.

The gravelly road led her straight through the town,

And she left without caring for aught she had seen.

It was hasty and new, hardly better than hovels,

Thrown up by the refugees fleeing the storm,

And swelling each day with fresh boats from Gwynedd.

She could blend in and vanish, if not for her plaids,

But those were so ragged the pattern was blurred.

She hoped that were true; then they'd leave her alone.

The country was crawling with farmers and guards;

There was so much to do in this wilderness land!

And no one paid heed to a ragged young girl;

There were too many like her to worry for one.

She followed the road by the banks of Elorn,

As it climbed through the mountains so much like her own,

And at length did arrive at the gates of Caer Lache,

Where a soldier she recognized called her by name.

The castle entire poured out on the green,

To rejoice in the safety of one they'd thought dead,

And at last came Meriadoc, ancient and hale,

To bestow his bright smile on the daughter he loved.

"Ah, my dear child, and where hast thou been!"

He cried in a voice that did boom off the fells,

Then he swept her up high with a hug like a bear's.

He released her at last and the whole Caer fell silent,

While Sarah related the tale of her deeds.

Of Guillaume she spoke not, for that was her treasure;

A secret she guarded with jealousy deep.

When she finished with speaking Meriadoc cried,

"Ah, my fair daughter, thou'rt truly my child!"

And the crowd roared approval that meant not a thing.
You know not the half of it, Sarah did think,
And smiled with her secret that no one could guess.
Then Meriadoc led all the court to the hall,
And commanded a feast to be set on the board,
In honor of Sarah, the bravest of Celts.
She was clothed in fresh dresses and jewelry bright;
Her long hair she brushed till it shone in the torches,
And she danced in the ballroom the waltzes and reels,
She'd learned in Caer Roderick's ancient stone halls.
The floor was a swirling of color and light,
A bed of bright flowers in form of the dancers,
Who laughed in high spirits to kiss her soft hand.
She danced for them all with a flush on her cheeks,
Till it seemed the whole world had its eyes on her back,
And the music poured through her like rivers of song,
That flowed in her body and spirit with love,
And the party would last till Eternity came,
While she danced through the night with her dearly Beloved.

But he was not there.

She stopped with a jerk as the thought grabbed her breath.
The party went on in its colorful loveliness,
Fragrant with sachets of roses and tea,

But Sarah walked slowly to stand by the wall,
And sit on a chair where her watered silk dress,
Fell down in soft folds like a stream to the floor.
The dancers could see her, and worried, she knew;
She would ruin the party for all if she stayed,
So she slipped from the room with a whisper of silk,
And found the thin stair that did climb to the tour.
There did she sit in the deep autumn dark,
Where none could behold her save mountains and stars.
She looked to the north where the sea stretched away,
In a shimmer of blue toward the Cambrian coast,
Where Guillaume still remained, perhaps; she knew not.
She never had asked, and now 'twas too late.
She cast down her face and then wept in the dark.
And she climbed the high tour every morning and eve,
To look out and long till her hope crumbled down,
But no one did come, or behold her alone,
Till Winter swept down on the hills of Bretagne,
And the mountains were coated with sheets of blue ice.
The days stretched as long as a wool spindle-thread,
And there she remained (so she thought), for all time.

Canto VII

But Fate is a mistress who plays many cards,

And Love is the master of all he surveys.

Though Sarah knew not that Guillaume loved her still,

And he dared not to hope that her heart might have changed,

Yet they both lived in love unbroken and sure,

Till at last he could bear it no longer.

So Guillaume did set out on an icy cold day,

In the depths of December when all things lay still,

Asleep under frost till the new year should come.

And he rode from Anjou to the hills of Bretagne,

Forsaken and empty of all men and beasts.

Long did he search for the maiden he loved,

For he thought in his heart he might ask just once more,

For her love and her hand, if her father approved.

And therefore he rode through the cold and the dark,

For many a day, till he almost despaired.

But then on the eve of Midwinter's Day,

He crossed the chill stream of the River Elorn,

And climbed a tall hill enshrouded with snow.

From the summit he looked to the north far away,

And beheld there a tower that stood tall and proud,

And lights and warm fire in the keep down below.

Guillaume was sore tired and chilled to the marrow,

And welcomed the sight of the castle right gladly,

Thinking at first he would ask there for shelter,

And room for the night, till morning should come.

For a chill salt fog crept close on his heels

Up the dark narrow vale from the cold grey sea,

Bright where the moon glinted soft on its edge,

And soon all things would be wrapped in its folds.

But then he espied a small figure alone,

Atop the tall tour neath the bright silver moon.

He knew it was Sarah the instant he saw,

And his heart beat so fast it was like unto bursting.

Then he spurred his tired horse to a gallop downhill,

And he came to the keep of Meriadoc quickly.

The guards let him in, a lone man and his horse,

And he left his bay charger in care of the ostler.

Then he ran to the hall where he found an old woman

And begged of her quickly to know how he might

Find the stairs to the tour before night fell at last.

A quizzical look did she give him indeed,

But she asked him no questions, and told him the way.

Then Guillaume climbed the steps to the platform above,

And found the door open with snow drifting in.

He crept to the opening quiet and slow,

Lest he startle the one who stood gazing alone.

For he heard the soft words of a half-uttered prayer,

And his name he heard whispered in longing.

Then the Prince of Anjou forsook all his caution,

Still sodden and cold from the fog and the snow,

And entered the tour where the Celt maiden stood,

And called out her name in great joy.

Then Sarah looked back, and their gaze met at last,

And for long neither one said a word.

Then he took her pale hand, and she turned up her face,

And they kissed by the light of the moon on the snow.

Now all has been said of Guillaume of Anjou,

And of Sarah Cymru, his Celt maiden bride,

Who loved long ago when the world was yet young,

In the snow-shrouded hills of distant Bretagne.

She stood on a tour in les Montagnes d'Arrée,
With snow in her hair and the ice at her feet,
Gazing through tears to the north over sea,
In the Celtic-plaid robes of a Princess Gwynedd.

She stood all alone in the evening to cry,
Where the moon on the drifts was as blue as her eyes,
Reflecting the winter that filled her inside,
And the midnight snow fell soft on her head.

She stood on her tour in les Montagnes d'Arrée,
As the bright salt fog rolled in from the sea,
And shrouded her longing so fully that she
Stood crushing her nails in her palms till they bled.

And she whispered a prayer with frost at her lips,
While the blood on her fingers trickled to drip,
And freeze on the stones like icicle chips,
But none could attend to the words that she said.

She stood in the wilderness aching alone,
With only the sighs of les Rapides d'Elorn,
To sing Brython songs for a maiden forlorn,
Whose heart still abode in the airs of Clwyd.

She stood on her tour in les Montagnes d'Arrée,
With snow in her hair her prayers to speak,
But none could have listened, for Winter was deep,
And even the wind on the summits lay dead.

But I know the words that she whispered that night,
In the fog and the darkness without any light,
And I prayed for the love that I saw in her eyes,
For all that it meant, and to all it has led,

Since that midwinter's night in les Montagnes d'Arrée,
When she whispered her prayers, unknowing, to me,
And turned from her gazing at long last to see,
The one who heard all, on that night in Bretagne.

French Translation Notes:

1: "I adore thee, my love and my life"

2: "My dear"

3: "If you wish, dearest one"

4: "Ah, I wish you great joy, my son!
Listen, therefore, while I sing of wisdom;
Love and life and your dreams and the Truth,
Only these are worthy to love in the end:
When life is easy, let the good times roll!
Remember true love can never die."

5: "The flowers are wild, and red in the rain,
But beautiful, when the world is dreary and gray.
I clasp their beauty tightly to my heart,
Here in the rain without the lady I love.
And I sing to myself in this far distant land,
Of you, the beautiful girl with my heart in her hand.
It's hard, and my blue eyes are gray like the rain,
That falls cold and sorrowful in this desolate place.
Ah, hear me, my love; my heart is broken!
But I will love you truly forever and ever. . ."

6: *Ex post facto* – "After the fact"

Author's Note:

As I wrote and edited these stories, at first it seemed that they had very little in common with each other. They were written at different times and for different reasons, over the course of several years.

In several of them you will find a strong flavor of Celtic mythology. For *Bran the Blessed*, in particular, I acknowledge a deep debt to several old Welsh and Irish legends. I have taken the liberty of adapting and blending the various stories considerably, but the original seeds are still clear, I think. *The Ballad of Sarah de Bretagne* is also set in Wales and Ireland, and partly in northwestern France. It has a germ of historical reality, namely the settling of Brittany (Bretagne) by Celtic peoples during the early Middle Ages, written in a style somewhat like the chanted tales of that period, when most stories were memorized by wandering bards rather than being written down.

In other stories, such as *Singing Wind*, there are echoes of Native American folk tales of the

South, although, again, greatly modified from the original.

Of the other tales I have little to say, since hopefully they speak for themselves. The various idea-germs and influences that led to them are probably of more interest to me than they are to anyone else. *The Keeper of Songs* came first from a dream I had. *Jacob Have I Loved* came originally from the circumstances of two brothers I once knew in high school. *The Way of Zoë* came to me as an image of the Tree. And finally, *The Land of Fear* came in the beginning from eating fried alligator at the Four States Fair in Texarkana, Arkansas. Story-seeds often grow in the strangest ways once they sprout.

As I read, I came to realize that all these tales are love stories. Whether it be love of a brother for a sister, a father for a son, a man for a woman, or a girl for her people or her God, they all contain the common theme of love. Equally, they are all tales of grace, in which the providence of God is clearly displayed. Thus the subtitle, *Seven Tales of Love and Grace*.

The main title, *Beneath a Star-Blue Sky*, was chosen because the majority of these tales were first told in some form as bedtime stories or campfire tales in the summer, and only much later were they set down on paper. Storytelling is a fluid art, in which the response of the listener has much to do with the final form of the tale. For that reason, there are a number of people I would like to thank for assisting me with this book:

Nathan, Elisabeth, Mathew, Cody, Zach, and Brandon, for listening to these tales and contributing some of their own ideas to them, and for making it all worthwhile in the first place. I can truthfully say that this book would never have been written without them.

Sarah, for leading me to love French ballads and Celtic mythology. To know her was to love her, and wherever she may be I wish her well.

And, as always and above all, thanks are due to God for making it all possible. No story is worth writing in which He is not the center. Blessed be He.

William Woodall
December 18, 2008

Character names

Brandon- Celtic warrior and saint

Delores – Sad, sorrowful

Nathan - Gift

Elisabeth – Consecrated to the Lord

Guillaume – Defender, protector

Jacob – In Genesis, the father of Joseph.

Joey – the best loved son of Jacob.

Sarah - Princess

Ulysses – Hater

Zoë - Life

Place names

Anjou- a northwestern province of France

Bretagne- northwesternmost peninsula of France

Cambria, Cymru- ancient names for Wales

Clwyd- a province of Wales

Eyre, Erin- ancient names for Ireland

Gwynedd- the northern part of Wales

Le Havre- city on the northern coast of France

Snowdon- a mountain in northern Wales

Toledo- city in Spain famous for its steel

About the Author:

William Woodall is a teacher, author, and businessman, with deep roots in the evangelical Christian community. His self-described literary influences include C. S. Lewis, J. R. R. Tolkien, and George MacDonald. He is the author of two novels, *The Prophet of Rain* and *Cry for the Moon*. This is his first collection of short stories. Mr. Woodall lives in western Arkansas.

Breinigsville, PA USA
05 December 2009
228670BV00001B/4/P